W9-BEK-920

"I was hired to protect you, not sleep with you."

Brad's words hit Carlotta like bullets.

"Why are you trying to hurt me?" she asked shakily. "Last night you told me you liked me, and touched me as if you wanted me."

"I decided that discretion was the better part of valor," he replied coolly.

"So what's that supposed to mean?" she demanded sharply. Was there no way through his steely defenses? "Don't talk to me in riddles."

"All right, you asked for it," he said harshly. "This is as straight and as basic as I can get. I decided not to betray Mason J. Burr's trust in me by making love to his daughter."

Carlotta flinched. She couldn't help it even though she guessed he was deliberately trying to antagonize her. "Was that the only reason why you didn't come to me last night?"

"Yes," he admitted slowly between taut lips. "Now go."

FLORA KIDD had a romantic dream—to own a sailboat and learn how to sail it. That dream came true when she found romance of another sort with a man who shared her love of the sea and became her husband and father of their four children. A native of Scotland, this bestselling romance author now lives in New Brunswick, one of Canada's maritime provinces, with the sea on her doorstep.

Books by Flora Kidd

HARLEQUIN PRESENTS
577—TEMPTED TO LOVE
592—DARK SEDUCTION
643—TROPICAL TEMPEST
657—DANGEROUS ENCOUNTER
682—PASSIONATE PURSUIT
729—DESPERATE DESIRE
756—THE OPEN MARRIAGE
771—FLIGHT TO PASSION
834—A SECRET PLEASURE
848—THE ARROGANT LOVER
970—PASSIONATE CHOICE
995—THE MARRIED LOVERS

HARLEQUIN ROMANCE
2146—TO PLAY WITH FIRE
2228—THE BARGAIN BRIDE

Don't miss any of our special offers. Write to us at the following address for information on our newest releases.

Harlequin Reader Service
901 Fuhrmann Blvd., P.O. Box 1397, Buffalo, NY 14240
Canadian address: P.O. Box 603,
Fort Erie, Ont. L2A 5X3

FLORA KIDD

masquerade marriage

Harlequin Books

TORONTO • NEW YORK • LONDON
AMSTERDAM • PARIS • SYDNEY • HAMBURG
STOCKHOLM • ATHENS • TOKYO • MILAN

Harlequin Presents first edition November 1987
ISBN 0-373-11024-3

Original hardcover edition published in 1987
by Mills & Boon Limited

Copyright © 1987 by Flora Kidd. All rights reserved.
Philippine copyright 1987. Australian copyright 1987.
Except for use in any review, the reproduction or utilization of
this work in whole or in part in any form by any electronic,
mechanical or other means, now known or hereafter invented,
including xerography, photocopying and recording, or in any
information storage or retrieval system, is forbidden without
the permission of the publisher, Harlequin Enterprises Limited,
225 Duncan Mill Road, Don Mills, Ontario, Canada M3B 3K9.

All the characters in this book have no existence outside the
imagination of the author and have no relation whatsoever to
anyone bearing the same name or names. They are not even
distantly inspired by any individual known or unknown to the
author, and all incidents are pure invention.

The Harlequin trademarks, consisting of the words
HARLEQUIN PRESENTS and the portrayal of a Harlequin,
are trademarks of Harlequin Enterprises Limited and are
registered in the Canada Trade Marks Office; the portrayal
of a Harlequin is registered in the United States Patent
and Trademarks Office.

Printed in U.S.A.

CHAPTER ONE

ALONE and feeling lonely, Carlotta Burr, only daughter of Texas oil tycoon Mason J. Burr II and heiress to his millions, sat at one of the tables on the patio at Brock's marina on the Caribbean island of Morunda and watched the crowd of people who were dancing on the deck.

It was New Year's Eve and the dancers were celebrating the fact. They were a mixed lot, owners of yachts, captains and crews off charter yachts, charterers, regular tourists from the States, Canada, Europe and South America, local merchants and business people. The colours of their skins ranged from the tapeworm whiteness of those who had just arrived from the frozen north, the lobster pink of the newly sunburned, through amber, café-au-lait and mahogany to deep, enduring ebony black. Of many ethnic origins and nationalities, they were united that night in their determination to welcome the New Year with noise and movement.

They had abandoned the bar, restaurant and patio to dance on the wooden deck that jutted out over water. Even waitresses and waiters were dancing to the music of drums, guitars and electric organ. Some couples shuffled, clinging to each other. Others preferred to be separate as they stamped, twisted and rocked, their feet thumping on wood. And all the time Carlotta watched.

No one looking at Carlotta would have guessed she was disconsolate. Sitting straight, looking like a pale moth in her dress of white chiffon, her golden hair, thick and rippling with natural waves, held back from her high brow with a black velvet band and swirling about her shoulders, one foot in its black velvet pump tapping in time to the music, she appeared cool, elegant and possibly a little haughty. Her expensive clothes and her cared-for beauty set her apart from the other people at the party, and were probably the reasons why she had not been asked to dance.

Yet there was one other person not dancing. He sat at another table a few yards away from Carlotta's, his long legs stretched under the small table. He was leaning back in the chair and his hands were in the pockets of his white trousers so that his elbows had pushed back the white suit jacket he was wearing. Under the jacket he wore a round-necked blue T-shirt, part of the uniform that the members of the crew of the motor yacht *Montezuma*, owned by Mason J. Burr, always wore.

For a few moments Carlotta let her attention leave the dancers and concentrate on the man at the other table. High forehead across which a straight lock of sun-bleached dark brown hair fell, bold nose, square jaw, he wasn't bad looking, she thought—and had always thought when she had seen him moving about the yacht. It was strange how often she had seen him when she had been ashore, had caught glimpses of him on Front Street sauntering along on the other side of the street from herself, or in a shop where she had stopped to buy something, or even at the casino—the other night he had been at the roulette table. And now he was here, a few yards away from her, yet not looking at her and, like her, he wasn't dancing.

Voices coming from inside the dining-room drew her attention away from him. A group of people had arrived to join in the festivities offered by the marina management for the celebration of the New Year. They were well dressed, the women in evening gowns and jewels, the men in white tuxedos and bow-ties. They were all well dined and well wined too, judging by their laughter and noisy voices.

As they approached the archway that gave access from the dining-room to the patio Carlotta recognised them and stiffened. One of the women was Phillida Chalmers, also from Dallas, Texas, and a cousin of Carlotta's stepmother, Cora. With Phillida was Gordon Chalmers, a business colleague of Mason J. Burr. The other couple were the Digbys from New York, and with them was their son, Bernard, the one person Carlotta had hoped to avoid meeting that night by dining at the unpretentious marina restaurant instead of going with him to the New Year's Eve dinner and ball at the International Hotel, Morunda's most luxurious and exclusive rendezvous.

On sudden impulse, driven by her intense dislike of Bernard as well as a certain flicker of panic, Carlotta sprang to her feet and went over to the man who was lounging at the other table. She sat down on the chair next to his.

'The music has changed. They're playing a

slow waltz for the end of the old year,' she whispered, leaning close to him, her shoulder touching his. 'Please will you dance with me?'

He turned his head slowly. To her surprise his eyes were dark brown, widely spaced and long-lashed; for some reason she had expected him to have grey or light blue eyes. His thick, slightly peaked eyebrows lifted in surprise.

Behind her she heard Bernard's voice, too jovial, too loud, wine-slurred.

'Please,' she whispered. 'Please dance with me. I need your help.'

Surprise was followed by a frown. For one impatient moment she thought he was going to refuse. Then suddenly he smiled, his eyes glinted and his generously curved lips parted to show strong white teeth. Attractive dents appeared in his lean cheeks.

'OK. Let's dance,' he said softly.

They stood up together and walked to the edge of the patio. Bernard called to her.

'Hey, Carlotta,' he shouted above the sound of the music, and there was a clatter as he tipped over one of the wrought-iron chairs in his haste to detain her.

'Quick.' Carlotta took hold of her companion's hand and pulled him with her down the shallow steps to the deck. Turning to him, she lifted her arms and linked her fingers together behind his neck. 'Hold me close,' she murmured. 'Hold me as if you're used to dancing with me, as if we've known each other for a long time. I don't want to talk to him. I don't want to have anything to do with him. He's a brute, an animal, after one thing only, and I'm at my wits' end wondering how to fend him off, to get rid of him.'

To her great relief, her partner didn't argue. His hands curved to the shape of her waist, and his cheek, only slightly bristly with beard stubble, pressed against hers. His right leg pushed against her left leg and then they were off, moving in unison, drifting about the wooden boards among the other couples in time to the music of the Anniversary Waltz as played by the Caribbean combo.

'I suppose you know who I am,' Carlotta whispered. His ear was close to her lips and his skin smelt of scented soap. The heat of his hands at her waist in intimate contact penetrated through the thin stuff of her dress to her smooth skin.

'You're the daughter of Mason J. Burr II,' he replied. 'Owner of the yacht I'm crewing on. I guess you know I've been on the *Montezuma* for the past few weeks.'

'Of course I do. I wouldn't have asked you to dance with me if I hadn't known that. What's your name?'

'You can call me Brad.'

'I've seen you often, in places where I've been in the town. Have you been following me?' she asked.

'Why would I want to follow you?' he murmured. 'It's just been a coincidence that I've been in the same place that you have.'

'I suppose so.' They drifted some more among the other dancers. Then she said: 'Did you see the man who called out to me? Can you see him now?'

'Yes.'

'What's he doing?'

'He's standing at the top of the patio steps

and he's watching us.' He felt his shoulders shake as he laughed. 'He looks like a bull is supposed to look when it sees a red rag.'

'Bulls have poor eyesight,' she said seriously. 'It isn't the red colour that enrages them but any sudden movement that they can't define clearly. They charge at the movement because they're afraid.'

'And you should know, I suppose, being the daughter of a cattle rancher who also happens to be the president of a Texas oil company,' he remarked drily.

They turned slowly. Dancing in that way, in entire body contact with him, was soothing, thought Carlotta dreamily. She felt safe being held by him, safer than she had felt for a long time.

'Who's the bullish-looking guy, and why don't you like him?' Brad asked, his breath wafting some tendrils of her hair.

'He's Bernard Digby, and I've known him for years. I don't like him because he's been taking advantage of old acquaintance,' she replied, somehow not finding it strange to confide in him. 'He thinks that because we've known each other for a long time he can make love to me whenever he feels like it. The only way I've been able to fend him off is to tell him my husband will be here tonight. Now I'm sure he's come to this dance to find out if Kurt has arrived.' She pushed away from him a little so she could look up at his face. Dappled by the light that was shining out on to the deck though the wide windows of the restaurant, his features were ruggedly handsome. He looked tough and self-assured, capable of dealing with any surprising or even dangerous event.

'I gather Kurt hasn't turned up,' he remarked, taking hold of her in a more conventional way, his right arm around her waist, his hand resting against her back while he took her right hand in his left as he whirled her in a traditional waltz movement.

'No, he hasn't. And he won't be coming,' she replied curtly, thinking how well Brad could dance, as if he had taken lessons in ballroom dancing at some time, guiding her through the movements easily, actually controlling where and how she moved. The experience was new for her. She had never met nor danced with a man who had taken over the direction of her dancing.

'Then you're in a bit of a fix, aren't you, princess?' he taunted. 'Caught out in a lie.'

'Why do you call me "princess"?' she demanded.

'Everyone around here calls you that.'

'Why?'

'Probably because you behave and look as they imagine a princess should.'

'But . . . that's silly. I'm just an ordinary person. I'm just like the other women of my own age who are here. I like to dance and have fun.'

'No, you're not like them. You're rich, an heiress to millions of dollars. That sets you apart from them.' He swung her around expertly, and the full skirt of her dress billowed out. 'Is it because your husband hasn't turned up that you need my help?' he asked.

'Yes. Please try to understand. I only lied to

Bernard in self-defence. It was all I could think
of to disconcert him the other night.'

'What do you want me to do?'

'If Bernard comes over to us and starts being
a nuisance would you mind pretending you are
Kurt? It will only be for a few minutes.'

His eyebrows flickered in surprise and he
pulled her close to him again. The whirling waltz
steps stopped and they began the slow shuffle
that all the other dancers were doing and which
made it possible for them to talk without being
overheard.

'I don't get this,' he said. 'Where is your
husband? Have you left him? Or has he left
you? Are you divorced or going to be? Or is he
going to turn up eventually?'

'He isn't going to turn up, ever,' she said
coldly and flatly. 'He died soon after we were
married, in a hunting accident. Broke his neck.
You don't need to know any more than that.'

'Oh, yes, I do,' he retorted. 'I need to know
his last name if I am to pretend to be him even
for a few minutes. I know you as Carlotta Burr.
Didn't you change your last name when you
married?'

'Yes, I did.' She was glad, she decided, that
he hadn't bothered to commiserate with her over
Kurt's death, to be hypocritical about it. 'But I
decided to revert to Burr when I came out to
Morunda.'

'Kurt sounds German,' he went on in a brisk
businesslike manner, strange to find in a
deckhand, she thought suspiciously. 'Was he a
German?'

'He was Austrian. I met him at a horse show
he was jumping in,' she said.   'I was jumping

in the same show. His last name was Malden. You may have heard of him. He won a gold in the last Olympic equestrian events.'

'No, I haven't heard of him. I don't follow the horse-jumping shows or events closely,' he said drily. 'So Malden is your married name. Doesn't Bernard know that Kurt is dead?'

'You're very picky,' she complained. 'You don't have to know everything. Just pretend to be Kurt if Bernard comes over and tries to accost me. Believe me he's quite capable of cutting in and causing a scene if I refuse to dance with him. Especially if he's smashed—and I can tell he's been drinking.'

'Please excuse me for being "picky" as you call it, princess,' he retaliated. 'But I like to be prepared for any eventuality. You've just told me Bernard is an old acquaintance of yours, so why doesn't he know that Kurt is dead?'

'He doesn't know because the news of Kurt's death hasn't been spread to my American friends. Only my father knows, and he won't have told anyone. Bernard was even surprised to find me here when he arrived in Morunda last week. Now, please will you do as I ask and pretend to be Kurt if Bernard comes over?'

They made a few slow turns before he answered. Carlotta couldn't help wishing that they were dancing together because they wanted to be dancing together, that this close-contact waltzing was a dance of courtship which would lead on to . . . Heavens, what was she doing, letting her thoughts wander into the realms of fantasy?

'How much?' her partner said softly and succinctly in her ear.

'How much what?' Startled, she stiffened and pushed away from him again so she could see his face. His black-fringed dark eyes gazed down at her enigmatically.

'How much will you pay me for pretending to be your husband for a few minutes?' he asked smoothly.

'You'd want to be paid?' she gasped.

'I would. In US dollars, preferably. I never do anything for anyone for nothing,' he drawled. 'I'm a mercenary. My services are for hire only.'

A sense of deep disappointment washed through Carlotta, to be followed quickly by a feeling of cold cynicism. She should have known, she thought. Whenever other people met her they saw dollar signs immediately, and wondered how much they could take her for.

'You've already been hired by Skipper Atkins and through him by my father to serve as a crew on the yacht,' she reminded him icily. 'I don't see why I should pay you anything.'

'But when I was hired no mention was made of me having to pretend to be your husband for a few minutes,' he argued mockingly. 'Now, I value my state of single blessedness very highly. Pretending to be married to you would mean I'd have to give up that single state, so if you want me to do it you'll have to pay.'

Dismayed by his tough bargaining, Carlotta was silent as he whirled her around again. What should she do now? Go on with the idea? Tell him she was willing to hire him for the next half-hour for so many dollars? Or should she step back, ask him to forget she had ever approached him, stop dancing with him and turn to face Bernard's leers?

Before she could decide, the music stopped suddenly with a loud chord from the electric organ. It was midnight. The old year had gone and the New Year was in. Everyone was suddenly wishing everyone else a happy New Year and kissing. The hooters of cargo ships in the harbour were sounding and fireworks were shooting up into the sky to fall in coloured and blazing white showers of sparks above the black outlines of the hills. The band began to play *Auld Lang Syne* and everyone began to make circles holding hands. A heavy hand slapped down on Carlotta's bare shoulder and she gasped. Bernard's voice boomed.

'Happy New Year, Carlo,' he yelled. 'How about a kiss?'

He began to push between her and her partner. She could see his thick lips gleaming lasciviously and his protruding pale eyes leering at her. She began to back away from him but quite suddenly he was shoved back by her partner, who stepped up to her, swept her against him and kissed her hard on the lips.

'Happy New Year,' he whispered, his dark eyes dancing with wicked mockery when he raised his head.

'Who the hell is this guy?' Bernard demanded pompously.

'I'm Kurt Malden. Who are you?' said Carlotta's partner, much to her relief.

'I told you Kurt would turn up today, Bernie,' she said smiling brightly to hide the sudden laughter that was bubbling up inside her at the expression of amazement on Bernard's round, fleshy face. She thought he looked like a small boy who had just had his favourite toy taken away from him by another child. 'Are you having a good time?' she went on. 'We are. It's been great fun here . . .'

'So this is where you've been hiding this evening, Carlotta,' said another voice, a high-pitched woman's voice that Carlotta recognised only too well. Her heart beating twenty to the dozen, her cheeks flaming suddenly red, she turned to face Phillida Chalmers reluctantly. Tall and stately in a long blue gown, white curls glittering like frozen foam, blue eyes narrow between mascaraed eyelashes, Phillida was looking not at Carlotta but at the man standing close to her, his arm around her waist. 'We were expecting you to join us at the International for dinner,' Phillida went on rather reprovingly. 'You were invited, you know, but when you didn't turn up Bernie suggested we would find you here.'

For only a moment Carlotta panicked, and nearly gave in to the desire to run away from them all rather than continue with the masquerade which she had initiated only to protect her from Bernard. It would be crazy to go on with it. Then she caught sight of Bernard's face: he was leering at her sceptically as if he had guessed the truth about her dancing partner. That expression was all she needed to make her go on recklessly with the pretence without a thought as to any consequences that might arise.

'Hello, Phillida,' she replied lightly. 'I'd have come to dinner with you, only Kurt arrived.' She turned to Brad and gazed up at him, hoping that the expression on her face was appropriately adoring. 'Darling,' she murmured, feeling wild laughter spurting up inside her at her own daring in using the endearment to this stranger. 'I'd like you to meet Phillida Chalmers. Phillida, this is Kurt, my husband. He flew in from Europe this afternoon. When did you arrive on the island?'

'We flew from Miami this afternoon.' Phillida held out her right hand to Brad. 'So pleased to meet you, Kurt, at last. We have all heard of Carlotta's runaway marriage to you and wondered if we would ever be allowed to meet you.'

'I'm pleased to meet you, Mrs Chalmers,' said the counterfeit Kurt—and Carlotta was surprised to hear him speak with what could have passed as an Austrian accent.

Suddenly, behind her and Brad the circling dancers broke up into couples and singles again. There was a lot of cheering and people rushed towards the patio steps as they made for the bar where free champagne was being served to welcome the New Year.

'Well, really, what a lot of ruffians,' complained Phillida, grasping Bernard's arm to regain her balance when she was almost knocked down by one of the dancers. 'I can't think why you want to be here, Carlotta. We came over in two cars, so why don't you and Kurt drive with us to the villa, right now? It's so lovely up there on a moonlit night. We can talk without interruption and you can both stay the night. You know we have plenty of room . . .'

'Thank you for the kind invitation,' Brad spoke with cool authority, 'but Carlotta and I would prefer to go back to the yacht. We haven't been together for some weeks and we have some catching up to do, haven't we, *sweetheart*?'

His arm tightened around her waist and his

dark eyes slanted a sultry glance down at her upturned face. Again she felt the desire to laugh. She was enjoying deceiving Phillida and Bernard, both of whom she disliked so much, and there was a certain excitement in sharing the masquerade with someone as quick-witted and self-confident as Brad seemed to be.

'Yes, we have, darling,' she murmured and leaned her head against his shoulder as she smiled at Phillida. 'Please excuse us, both of you. We'd like to dance some more and then go to bed.'

'We could stay,' Bernard suggested quickly. 'It's more fun here, Phillida . . .'

'You can stay if you want, Bernie.' Phillida had to shout because the band had started up again, playing a boisterous Caribbean number with a strong rocking rhythm. 'I can't stand this noise and I'm sure Gordon and your parents can't either. We're leaving. Good night, Carlotta, Kurt. I'll come over to see you tomorrow.'

Turning on her heel Phillida marched towards the patio and was almost knocked down again as dancers rushed back to the deck to stamp and rock to the lively beat of the music. And suddenly Carlotta found herself whirling round and round securely held by her partner in the deception she had just enacted.

She was whirled away from the bewildered yet suspicious Bernard, guided expertly among the other dancers until they were all between her and Bernard. Right to the end of the deck she was whirled, to the place where the first concrete dock of the marina joined it, and the shadows of the marina buildings were thick and black.

They stopped dancing and stood still, both of them breathing hard, facing each other.

'Thanks,' said Carlotta when she had breath enough for speech. 'Thank you for helping out. Bernard's face was a picture when you said you were Kurt. He was absolutely stunned. I wanted to laugh so much.'

He let go of her and pushed his hands in his trouser pockets. There wasn't much light where they were standing, although beyond the shadows everything was silvered by the radiance of the full moon now sailing high in the clear midnight blue of the tropical sky. She could see that he was frowning at her.

'How . . . how much do you want me to pay you?' she asked, remembering his demand just before Bernard had wished her a happy New Year.

'That depends on how long you want the pretence to continue,' he replied curtly.

'What do you mean?' She spoke sharply. 'I told you it would be for a few minutes, for Bernard's benefit.'

'Then it was hardly wise of you to introduce me as your husband to Phillida Chalmers, was it? Especially since she's going to call to see you tomorrow.' His voice rasped drily. 'You're in it now, right up to your neck, *sweetheart*.' Sarcasm edged his voice as he spoke the endearment. 'It won't take long for her to find out I'm not your husband but only a deckhand on your father's yacht. And I wouldn't be surprised if your pursuer, Bernard, doesn't start checking on me tonight. All he has to do is go to the yacht and ask if Kurt Malden is on board. Hadn't you thought of that?'

'No, I hadn't,' she admitted frankly. She hadn't thought beyond the impulse that had led her to ask him to play the part of Kurt. Invaded by panic and a sort of moon-madness, she hadn't thought at all. 'I didn't think . . .'

'I bet you never do,' he interrupted unkindly. 'I bet you're always rushing into situations without thinking. I'd take a guess too that your runaway marriage to Kurt was one of them. It didn't work out the way you wanted so you rushed out of it, rushed back to Daddy, to his yacht where you could hide. Or thought you could hide, but unfortunately Bernard turned up and started to pester you!'

'Shut up,' she hissed furiously. 'You've no right to speak to me like that. No right to criticise me.'

'Excuse me.' His voice drawled mockingly. 'I forgot my position. I forgot I'm only one of your father's employees and likely to lose my job if he finds out from Skip Atkins that I've been impersonating your husband.'

'Oh, no!' Carlotta exclaimed. 'I don't want that to happen. I don't want Phillida or Bernard to find out I've deceived them. At least, not yet. And I don't want you to lose your job.' She broke off as she heard footsteps coming towards them. A high-shouldered, big-headed figure in a white tuxedo was coming towards them. 'Bernard. He's coming this way!' she whispered. 'What shall we do?'

For answer Brad seized her hand in a rough sinewy grasp and made for the steps that led down from the deck to the beach, pulling her after him.

CHAPTER TWO

BEFORE them the beach of yellow sand that curved around the head of the wide bay was lit by the moon. It was possible to walk along the sand to the town of Morrisburg, Morunda's capital and port, instead of going by road. Now, the lights from the houses and hotels in the town glittered like jewels against the dark slopes of the hills behind it, and fireworks sent up in celebration of the New Year blossomed in the sky, red, white and blue.

There were no shadows on the beach where Carlotta and Brad walked hand in hand. Anyone standing on the marina deck would see them.

'I should have guessed he wouldn't go to the villa with the others. I should have guessed he would stay around to spy on me,' Carlotta murmured bitterly. She glanced over her shoulder quickly. 'Oh, he's following us, coming down the steps.'

'He doesn't seem to be as stunned or as convinced as you'd hoped he would be,' said Brad calmly, not looking back at all, seeming completely unconcerned.

'I don't want him to start bothering us now,' complained Carlotta. 'Oh, let's hurry away from him.'

'No.' His grasp on her hand tightened. 'If we

start showing panic by running away from him
he'll guess he's on to something.' He swung her
round to face him. 'Best to do something to put
him off the scent. Such as this.'

Dropping her hand, he framed her face with
both his hands and before she could do or say
anything to stop him he kissed her. Her first
instinct was to resist, to push him away, but his
hands left her face and caught her wrists roughly.
He twisted her arms behind her back forcing her
body against his. While dancing with him she
hadn't objected to the close contact, but now
the roughness of his actions awoke an oft-
smothered memory within her. She shuddered
and stiffened.

At once he lifted his lips from hers and
whispered softly and sardonically. 'You're not
the most loving wife in the world, sweetheart.
How about relaxing a little and showing Bernard
just how glad you are that I've turned up tonight
and that I'm here to protect you from his over-
amorous attentions?'

One of his hands left her wrists and slid up
her back slowly, the heat of it seeming to burn
through the thin chiffon. His fingers wound in
her hair, grasping a bunch of the silky strands so
tightly that it would have hurt her to turn her
face away from his.

'Now, when I kiss you again, kiss me back,'
he whispered. 'I'm sure you really know how.'

His lips touched hers and she shuddered again,
not because she disliked the feel of his lips so
much but because ever since Kurt's horrible and
frightening mauling of her on their wedding
night she had hated being touched by a man.

Being kissed caused a cold, hard knot of loathing to form inside her.

'Kiss me,' Brad ordered again against her lips and held her closer to him. Closing her eyes tightly, she pressed her lips to his, then slowly raised her arms and put them round his neck. The hair at the back of his neck felt thick and silky.

It would be over soon, she told herself. It wasn't going to last for long, just long enough to convince Bernard that Brad was really her husband Kurt, and she was unprepared for the way Brad's lips began to move experimentally over hers, exploring their softness and then parting them so that his tongue could flicker briefly yet tantalisingly against the tip of hers. The teasing touch of his tongue seemed to send a scalding heat through her that melted the knot and danced flamelike through the lower part of her body. As he had suggested she relaxed against him and immediately her body was invaded by a host of new sensations. She felt the strong beat of his heart striking through to her breast, the pressure of his long fingers in one of her buttocks, the thrust of one of his knees between hers. From being a masquerade kiss, a pretence merely to convince Bernard, the embrace was fast developing into a sensuous experience that she was enjoying. Seduced by the warmth of his lips and the touch of his hands, she clung to him, licking his lips, savouring the taste of them, inhaling the scents of his skin and hair until she felt a little giddy.

As if he also sensed the kiss was going on too long and was possibly getting out of control, Brad lifted his head abruptly.

'OK, that will do,' he whispered scoffingly.
'No need to overact. Bernard's gone.'

His withdrawal and cool, mocking remarks
had a devastating effect on her. She felt as if she
had been rejected. Bewildered by the feeling,
her hands at her hot cheeks, she stepped back
from him quickly and glanced round. It was true
Bernard was no longer up there watching. Nor
was he walking towards them over the soft sand.
Bewilderment faded, its place being taken by
anger.

Turning to face Brad she raged in a whisper,
'Don't ever do that again. It wasn't necessary to
kiss me.' She wiped the back of her hand across
her bruised and trembling lips. 'I don't like
being kissed.'

'So it seems,' he retorted.

He was casual again, an unconcerned stranger,
hands in his trouser pockets and head bent so
that the long, recalcitrant lock of straight hair
slid forward on to his forehead. With one foot
he was pushing around a piece of dry, washed-
up seaweed. He was even whistling softly between
his teeth, the tune the band was playing now, a
song by Stevie Wonder, which was a favourite of
hers.

'*I just called to say I love you*.' The voices of
the dancers singing the popular lyric floated
down and Carlotta winced. Once she had believed
Kurt loved her. She had believed also that she
had loved him. Now she knew that there had
been no real love between them, but only
infatuation on her part and greed on his, both of
which had changed to hate and frustration under
pressure.

She glanced at Brad again. He had stopped

whistling and was no longer playing with the seaweed. Straight and still, he was watching her, his dark eyes pools of blackness in his moon-silvered face. She had the impression that he was watching her with concern and interest. But, then, he was probably only waiting to be paid, she thought wryly.

I'll see you tomorrow,' she said coolly. 'I'll pay you then. In American dollars, of course.'

She turned and walked back to the deck. Going up the steps she held her head high, her slim shoulders straight. The tempo of the music tempted her momentarily to join the dancers again, but the thought that Bernard might be among them, dancing either with one of the girls off the charter yachts or sitting on the patio, watching and drinking, deterred her.

Reaching the concrete dock where the *Montezuma* was tied up, she paused watching the dancers enviously, wishing she were one of them, wishing above all that she wasn't who she was. Wild impulses flitted through her mind. Ignoring them with difficulty, she turned and began to walk along the dock past the bows and sterns of the yachts tied up in the berths. Some boats were dark and deserted. Others had light streaming out from cabin windows and people sitting around in cockpits and on decks, talking, laughing, still welcoming the New Year. Several voices called out to her as she passed. Someone even invited her aboard to have a drink. Shaking her head in refusal, she walked on.

Behind her a pleasantly deep voice with an English accent said, 'Very sensible of you, if I may say so, to refuse any invitations at this hour and to return to the yacht.'

Brad caught up with her, loped along beside her.

'I don't really care what your opinion is of my behaviour,' she said haughtily. It was time to put him back in his place as a deckhand employed by her father. 'Please don't speak to me or walk with me. And you don't have to come back to the yacht with me.'

'I want to make sure you don't go out again tonight,' he replied. 'And that you won't involve me in any more pretences.'

She didn't answer him. It was becoming very clear to her that he was one of those odious people she couldn't possibly get the better of in a verbal exchange. She walked on towards the *Montezuma*. Seventy-five feet of gleaming white paint, stainless steel fittings and glass windows, a great white whale of a power cruiser, it tugged gently at the ropes that tied it to the dock.

The gate in the port rail was open. As Carlotta stepped through it on to the main deck, a man came out of the doorway of the main saloon. He was stockily built and dressed in white shorts and a white shirt.

'Good night, Skip,' Carlotta said, and made her way to the stairs that led to the lower deck, the after cabins and stateroom.

'Good night, miss.' Skipper Atkins, who had been captain of the yacht for the four years Mason J. Burr had owned it, was, as always, briskly polite. Before she reached the stairs she heard him say to the man who had been with her, 'I'd like a word with you, Brad. Something queer has happened.'

'All right. Be with you in a few minutes,' answered the deckhand, who didn't sound at all subservient. 'Just as soon as I've seen Miss Burr to her cabin.'

She swung to face him as he came after her.

'You don't have to see me anywhere,' she whispered angrily. 'I can look after myself. I'm grown up!'

'You could have fooled me—about being grown up, I mean,' he taunted and smiled at her, disconcerting her. There was something about the way he smiled at her that destroyed the desire to rebel against him. Instead, she discovered she wanted to please him by doing exactly what he suggested.

With a little exclamation of irritation she turned and ran down the stairs and along the narrow carpeted passage to her cabin. Opening the door, she stepped over the sill and into the room, slamming the door shut after her and leaning against it.

After a while, when nothing happened, she moved across to the porthole. It was slightly open and she could still hear the music from the deck. Her foot tapped in time to the beat and rebelliousness stirred within her again, an old, familiar restlessness. Now she was wishing she hadn't returned to the yacht but had joined the dancers. Or, better than going to the marina and perhaps running into Bernard, she wished she had gone along the beach to Morrisburg to dance there in one of the discothèques. If she hadn't been so bewildered by Brad's behaviour she might have persuaded him to go with her. They could have danced together all night until their feet and legs had ached if he hadn't kissed her.

She could still go into the town. She didn't need him around to escort her. Hardly had the

impulse flared up than she had spun around and
was on her way to the door. Her hand closed
around the brass knob. She pushed. The door
remained shut. She pushed again, her shoulder
against the panels. It didn't open. Yet it wasn't—
it couldn't possibly be locked! But if it wasn't
locked, why didn't it open?

Raising her clenched fists, she banged on the
door and shouted to be let out. Her horror of
being locked in or restrained in any way surged
through her and had to be expressed in violent
action. But for all the noise she made no one
came, and she realised that no one would hear
her. Skipper Atkins was in the saloon with Brad,
and perhaps Jilly, the first mate, was there too.
Willy, the other deckhand, was probably ashore
still celebrating the New Year.

But there was still the bathroom door. Of
course! Why hadn't she thought of that instead
of wasting breath and energy banging on this
door! *I bet you never think*. Brad's jeer rang
through her mind. Perhaps he was right. She
didn't think. She'd never had to.

She flitted over to the doorway that led into
the small bathroom attached to her cabin. Across
the tiny room she went to the outer door, turned
its knob and pushed. The door remained closed,
Golden-brown, like the door of her cabin, shiny
with varnish, it was solid and it didn't open. It
too was locked.

But who would lock both doors from the
outside? Had Brad locked them? Had he followed
her after all, even though she had ordered him
not to see her to her cabin, and had he locked
her in?

How? How could he, who was only a

deckhand, have the keys to lock the doors? Only if Skip Atkins had given him the keys. Only if the keys had been taken from inside the doors at some time. That is if there had been any keys in the locks. She didn't really know if there had because she had never looked. She had never thought to lock her doors at night or at any other time.

Returning to the cabin, she flung herself down on the wide bunk and kicked off her velvet pumps. The music from the marina drummed through her head, and in an agony of frustration she beat at the pillow under the bunk cover with her fists.

Why had she been locked in? Why? Who had locked her in? If Brad had locked her doors, on whose orders had be been acting? What was it Skip Atkins had said to him? That something queer had happened? Something to do with her? Had the skipper ordered the deckhand to lock her in her rooms for the night? Who would give the skipper orders to lock her in if something occurred that made it necessary, for her own safety? Only the owner of the yacht, of course, her father.

Carlotta sighed irritably and shifted into a more comfortable position, her head on the pillow. She knew her father was concerned about her welfare. He always had been. It had been his idea that she should come to Morunda and stay on the *Montezuma* instead of going to Texas. She had phoned him from England, from the home of his cousin Grace Heward where she had gone after she had left Kurt.

'I'll advise Atkins that you're coming,' Mason J. Burr had said, delighted that she had left

Kurt. 'Stay on the yacht as long as you like. Stay there until I can get away and fly down to see you. And don't tell anyone you're going there!'

'I'll have to tell Grace,' she had interrupted him. 'She'll want to know where I'm going.'

'That's OK. Grace won't tell anyone. She's as close as they come, respects privacy. I want it kept out of the gossip columns, sugar. I don't want anyone to know where you are and above all I don't want that creep Kurt following you.'

It was then she had told him about Kurt's unexpected death in a fall when he had been training a new horse. The news of the accident had filtered through to her along the grapevine of the show-jumping community. Since no one had known she had married Kurt Malden secretly, information of his death had not been communicated to her directly, and apparently he hadn't told anyone back in Vienna that he had married the Burr heiress.

Although she had left Kurt the day after they had married and had been determined to divorce him somehow as soon as she could, the news that he had died with such abrupt violence had shocked Carlotta severely and she was sure that if she hadn't had the support of Grace she would have been ill. Coming as it had so soon after that other shock, the shock of her wedding night, the news could have caused her to have a nervous breakdown, if Grace, calm, shrewd Grace, hadn't pointed out to her that Kurt's death could have happened anyway, even if he hadn't been married to her, that she should put all past mistakes behind her and look forward to the future.

Restlessly she flung over on to her back. It was to avoid moments like these when she relived the recent past that she had helped Grace at the stables in Berkshire while she had stayed there. Every day she had mucked out stables, groomed horses or gone riding as far as she had been able, trying to tire herself so that she would fall asleep as soon as her head hit the pillow.

Here too, staying on the yacht, she had indulged in physical activities every day, swimming and snorkelling, playing tennis, wind-surfing, and dancing at the various hotels and discos, doing anything to stop herself from remembering the mistake she had made in marrying Kurt.

She had first met him four years ago when she had been eighteen and jumping at a horse show in the States. It had been her first venture into international show-jumping events. After that first one, flushed with success, encouraged by her father and grandmother, backed by plenty of money and owning fine horses, she had gone on to compete in many events in the States and Europe. At all of them she met Kurt.

He had been ten years older than her, coolly sophisticated, with smooth, jet-black hair and black eyes. He had told her that he was descended from a long line of Austrian aristocrats and he had won more awards for show jumping than she could remember.

When he had shown an interest in her she had been flattered. Hero-worship had developed rapidly into infatuation for him, and so when he had proposed marriage to her last September she had been so delighted that she had accepted his proposal immediately.

They had been in Vienna at the time, both attending some horse trials there. She had phoned her father and told him her news. Mason J. Burr had flown out to Vienna to meet Kurt, had taken an instant dislike to the accomplished equestrian and had forbidden Carlotta to marry him.

'You can't forbid me to marry,' she had stormed at him. 'I'm twenty-one, nearly twenty-two. I can marry Kurt if I want and you can't stop me.'

'All I'm asking you to do, honey, is to slow down a little. To think about it. Marriage is a serious step and you don't know this guy too well.'

'I've known him for nearly four years.'

'But only off and on. You've only met him at these horse affairs. You know nothing about his background . . .'

'Yes, I do. I do! I know he comes from a very good family.'

'Have you met any of them?'

'No. All his nearest relatives are dead. He . . . he's alone in the world. And I don't need to know about his background. I love him and I'm going to marry him no matter what you say about him. You're always the same. You always dislike any guy who takes an interest in me.'

'Bide your time, then,' he had argued, quite reasonably she realised now, looking back. 'Get engaged but don't get married in a hurry. Get to know him better. You might change your mind.'

'No. I won't. I'll never change my mind, and

I'm going to marry him as soon as I can and you can't do anything about it.'

Mason J. Burr hadn't stayed to argue. He had left Vienna abruptly and she had lied to Kurt, had told him that her father had agreed to their marriage. Within a week they had flown to Paris and had been married there in a secret civil ceremony. Before the ceremony she'd cabled her father to inform him of the wedding, inviting him to attend. He hadn't flown to Paris but had sent a cable in return. It had been waiting for her when she and Kurt had arrived at the honeymoon suite, in a luxury Paris hotel, that she had booked.

'If you marry Malden you allowance will automatically stop and I shall cut you out of my will.'

The stark message of her father's cable seemed to be branded on her mind. She had shown the cable to Kurt. It had been a foolish thing to do, she could see that now. It would have been better to have waited a while, until the marriage had been consummated, until they had settled into a relationship.

She would never forget the effect of the cable on Kurt. Never. The elegant aristocrat had disintegrated before her eyes. He had become a foul-mouthed bully who had accused her of leading him to believe she was wealthy and would always be wealthy, of trapping him into a marriage he didn't want now that he knew she would be disinherited.

'But . . . I thought . . . we married today because we . . . we love each other,' she had stammered and going to him had put her arms around him. 'Money isn't all that important . . .'

'No. Not to someone like you who has always had more than enough,' he had snarled at her. 'As for love.' He had laughed jeeringly at her. 'There's no such thing.'

'I love you. I wouldn't have married you if I didn't,' she had argued.

'Rubbish, romantic rubbish,' he had jibed. 'A cover-up women like you use to disguise sexual desire. You've deceived me, trapped me with your wealth, so you're going to find out now just what you've let yourself in for . . .'

What had happened next she had been trying to forget ever since. Oh, their marriage had been consummated all right, in the worst possible way, in a spirit of revenge. Kurt had taken her without tenderness or respect, without love, and next morning early, before he had been awake she had packed her bags, paid the bill and left Paris to fly to London. She had gone straight to the home of Grace Heward.

Three months had gone by since that awful night in Paris and she still felt frozen inside, still stiffened and retreated when a man showed an interest in her, when someone like Bernard came on to her . . .

She turned again on to her side and closed her eyes. The music from the marina deck beat through her brain and suddenly she was dancing again with Brad, feeling safe in his arms as he whirled her around. She was spinning down and down into darkness, around and around. She fell asleep.

CHAPTER THREE

HAVING been lulled to sleep by the distant throb of drums and guitars, Carlotta was awakened by the closer, more workmanlike throb of the *Montezuma's* powerful Rolls-Royce engines. Without opening her eyes, she stretched lazily and wondered vaguely why they had been started up. Then she turned over, snuggled her head into the pillow and tried to go to sleep again.

There was a knock on the door of the cabin. She opened her eyes, aware of a vague memory of the door having been locked from the outside when she had tried to open it last night. Knuckles rapped on the door again. She sat up and realised she had slept on top of the bunk cover and that she was still wearing the white chiffon dress. This morning it looked like a rag.

She swung her legs off the bed and went towards the door intending to shout through the thick wood that she couldn't open the door because it was locked from the outside. She had almost reached it when the brass knob turned slowly and the door was pulled open. In the passageway outside, Jilly Atkins, the skipper's wife who was also first mate and cook, stood, her round, cheerful face puckered in a slight frown of puzzlement. She was dressed in the crisp, white shorts and navy blue T-shirt that all

the *Montezuma's* crew wore as their uniform,
and on the palm of one hand she was carrying a
small, round tray on which there stood a large
glass of orange juice, the drink that Carlotta
preferred when she woke up.

'Good morning, miss,' Jilly said, a bright smile
replacing the frown, 'and a happy New Year.'

'Thanks, Jilly. And a happy New Year to
you.' Carlotta took the tray and put it on a shelf
beside the bunk. She was aware that Jilly was
now looking in surprise at the creased and rag-
like chiffon dress. 'I was so tired after dancing
last night,' she was quick to explain, 'that I lay
down and fell asleep before I had time to
undress. I've only just woken up. What time is
it?'

'Nine o'clock, give a minute or two either
way,' replied Jilly. Her brown hair was cut very
short, shingled at the back and spraying out in
all directions on top of her head. Small gold
buttons decorated the lobes of her ears. Not
very tall, she was broad-shouldered and athletic-
looking, and Carlotta knew after spending only
a few weeks on board that Jilly was a competent
and fearless navigator and sailor, as well as an
excellent gourmet cook.

'Why are the engines going?' Carlotta asked,
after sipping some of the juice. Freshly squeezed
from Florida oranges, as she liked it, the juice
pricked her palate, washing away the dryness
that had developed in her mouth during sleep.

'The skipper has decided to take the ship for a
spin through the islands. He'll tell you all about
it when you come up for breakfast,' replied Jilly.
'He said it's time to blow the cobwebs out of
them, that they've been idle long enough.'

'Good idea,' murmured Carlotta, then added quickly as Jilly moved towards the door, 'wait a minute, please. How did you open the door just now? Do you have a key to unlock it?'

Jilly's eyes opened wide in surprise. She looked down at the brass knob and the brass-edged keyhole below it.

'It wasn't locked, miss. The key is usually on the inside of the door.' She looked back at Carlotta, her eyes puzzled. 'Did you lock the door, miss? After you came in?'

'No. And to tell the truth I've never noticed a key in the lock on the inside of the door. I've never even thought of locking the door. But last night when I came back from the restaurant I decided to go out again. I couldn't because the door was locked. From the outside. I banged and shouted but no one heard me. It was the same with the door from the bathroom.'

'Well, I never,' exclaimed Jilly, whose real name was Jillian. Like her husband, she was English, and had once told Carlotta that she was born and grew up in the city of Liverpool. Although she hadn't lived in England for several years she still had a Liverpool accent, and her speech was sprinkled with English idioms. Before applying for the jobs of captain and first mate on the *Montezuma*, she and Stan had both worked on a British cruise ship, he as first mate and she as chief stewardess.

'Sometimes I've noticed that the doors on the yacht stick,' she continued now, pleasantly, as if wishing to reassure Carlotta. 'They swell in the heat and humidity. If you'd given the door a good shove . . .'

'I did.' Carlotta cut in impatiently. 'It wasn't

sticking. Neither of them were. They were locked.'

'Then you'd better tell Stan about it,' said Jilly. 'He might have locked them.' She grinned. 'I wouldn't put it past him,' she added mysteriously. 'Excuse me, now, miss. I must go and cook the breakfast.'

Jilly left the cabin and Carlotta finished drinking her orange juice and put the glass back on the tray.

Dragging the black velvet band from her head, she shook out her hair. Like a cloak of golden silk it swirled about her face and shoulders. Noticing the black velvet pumps she had kicked off the night before, she picked one of them up and examined it curiously. Grains of sand clung to the soft velvet. So she hadn't imagined all that had happened. She had walked down to the beach from the marina deck and she had been kissed, very thoroughly and quite unnecessarily kissed by a stranger.

Dropping the shoe, she stripped off the white dress and her underclothing and ran nude into the bathroom. A few minutes later, after a quick hot shower, she returned to the main cabin, her wet hair clinging to her body. She dressed quickly again in white shorts and a scarlet shirt, wound her still wet hair up into a knot on top of her head, found her sunglasses, slipped on sandals, and with a scarlet leather handbag slung over one shoulder she left the cabin and went up to the main deck and the saloon.

Through the wide windows of the saloon she could see the buildings of the marina hotel appearing, white walls and red roof shining in the bright sunlight, glowing against the green scrub of cacti and small bushes that covered the high hillside behind them. The expanse of water between the yacht and the land was a brilliant jade green glittering with yellow sunbeams.

In one corner of the big saloon there was a dining area. A cushioned settee berth covered in biscuit-coloured tweed curved about an oval table that was already set with two place mats, cutlery and blue plates. Skipper Atkins entered the saloon and came over to the table. He was carrying his peaked cap under one arm and, watching him from her corner of the settee, Carlotta thought, as always, that he and Jilly must have come out of the same mould. They were the masculine and feminine versions of the same character, both short and energetic, both pale-eyed and brown-haired, both speaking with the same accent.

'Good morning, miss.' Stan Atkins sat opposite her, on one of the upholstered chairs which were attached to the floor. Since she had arrived on the yacht he had breakfasted with her every morning. It seemed to be some sort of custom for the captain of the yacht to take the first meal of the day with the owner or representative of the owner, and she wondered who had started the custom on the *Montezuma*—her father, or this sharp-eyed Englishman?

'It's a lovely day,' he said cheerfully after she had acknowledged his greeting. 'I hope you didn't have anything planned to do ashore this morning. I suppose I should have asked you before we cast off from the dock.'

'Yes, you should have,' retorted Carlotta, but she smiled at him as she spoke. 'But I'm quite

happy to get away from the marina this morning.
Are you aiming for anywhere in particular?'

'Not really. I thought I'd leave that to you,
miss. Where would you like to go?'

'St Phipps,' said Carlotta without hesitation.
St Phipps was a sister island to Morunda, and
both came under the same government. 'The
Bay of Doves. Have you ever heard of Stewart
Stenson?'

'Wasn't he that crazy recluse who inherited
millions from his grandfather and then went
about spending all the money on nutty projects?
A bit like Howard Hughes?'

'That's right. He bought a whole headland in
the Bay of Doves, built a house there and
landscaped the area with all kinds of tropical
trees and shrubs,' said Carlotta. 'It's now called
Stenson Point after him, and the father of a
friend of mine from Dallas has bought the estate.
I'd like to see it. Is the anchorage in the Bay of
Doves any good? I mean, is there enough depth
of water for the *Monte*?' She used her father's
shortened and affectionate version of the yacht's
name.

'There's enough,' said the skipper. 'The
entrance is a bit tricky, strewn with rocks, but
once you're in you can anchor close to the shore.
There's good snorkelling too, off the Point of
Doves, opposite Stenson Point.'

'So can we go there now and stay the night
there?' Carlotta was eager. It was just possible
her friend Tizzy Carter, whose father had bought
the Stenson estate, might be there, and it would
be good to see Tizzy again. Nearly two years
had passed since she had last seen her friend:
two years during which she had gone with Kurt

from one equestrian competition to the next, with never a thought for old friends.

'Of course we can. We can go wherever you want. You're the boss when your dad isn't on board,' replied the skipper with a twinkle.

'Am I?' Carlotta spoke drily. 'I wonder. I got the impression last night that my father's wishes and orders where I'm concerned stretch right down here from Texas.'

'Miss Burr couldn't open the doors of her cabin last night,' Jilly said, having overheard Carlotta's remarks as she brought two silver serving dishes to the table and set them down. 'She couldn't get out.'

'Oh? When was this?' queried the skipper, lifting off one of the covers. 'Mmm. Bacon and kidneys. Help yourself, miss.'

'After I'd returned to the yacht. Just after I'd seen you,' replied Carlotta, serving herself. 'I decided to go out again but couldn't get out. Both doors were locked from the outside.'

'They were probably sticking,' said the skipper blandly, heaping food on to his plate. 'I'll have Willy look at them.'

'They weren't sticking. They were locked,' Carlotta insisted, frowning at him fiercely, her slanting dark eyebrows taking on even more of a slant, her lower lip thrusting out.

The skipper didn't bat an eyelid. Round and clear his eyes looked straight back at her.

'The keys to the cabin doors are always on the inside for the use of the occupants of the cabins, so that they can lock their doors at night after they have retired to bed or, if they wish, to lock from the outside when they go ashore and take the keys with them,' he said coolly. 'Now, are you sure you didn't lock the doors yourself when you returned to the cabin and forget they were locked when you tried to go out?'

'Oh, come on, Skip, I'm not that stupid,' Carlotta retorted. 'I didn't know there were any keys in the locks. I haven't noticed any since I came on the yacht this time and I've never noticed them before. I've never wanted to lock myself in or to lock the doors when I've left the ship. I guess I've always felt safe on board with you and Jilly and the crew. I guess I've always felt I could trust you all.'

'Hmm.' Jilly had returned with a coffee-pot and was pouring the liquid into their mugs. 'Maybe you're too trusting, miss, she said, looking severe. 'Now I'm not saying that Stan or I or the crew can't be trusted. We can. But when we're tied up at a dock it's easy enough for any stranger to walk aboard without us seeing him or her. Unless we kept a member of the crew always posted at the gate we could be boarded at any time. I think you should always lock your cabin doors. Don't you, Stan?'

'Do you lock yours when you go ashore or when you go to bed at night?' asked Carlotta, raising her eyebrows at them and they both had the grace to look disconcerted.

'No, we don't, miss. But it might be a good idea if we all did,' said Stan Atkins. 'I should have suggested it to you when you arrived, but I just assumed you'd be careful and lock your doors always. There's been a lot of theft and piracy in the islands—not so much here on Morunda or on St Phipps where there's full employment, thanks to the tourist trade, but on some of the other islands where the economy isn't so well developed and there's a lot of poverty.'

'We've even heard of murders,' Jilly added. 'And we've heard of a crew and yacht we know being hi-jacked by four armed men in the island of the Dominican Republic. They were forced to take the men to Puerto Rico.'

'Did they get to Puerto Rico?'

'They had a bad crossing in the Mona Strait and everyone was ill,' the skipper took up the story. 'Then the engine quit. The armed men took to the Zodiac dinghy at that point because they were only a few hundred yards from the coast. They forgot about the radio. The crew of the yacht radioed the American coastguard and when the armed men went ashore they found a welcoming party of coastguards waiting for them.' He paused, and then added, 'That little escapade ended safely for the skipper and crew of the yacht. But it might not have done. I think it would be best if you locked your doors, miss.'

'Well, I will in future,' said Carlotta. 'But you haven't told me who locked my doors last night. Did you? Or did you give orders to the deckhand I met ashore last night to lock them?'

'Excuse me, now, miss,' he said politely, rising to his feet. 'Time I got back to the wheelhouse. We're just about to clear the harbour bar and I'd like to set the ship on course for St Phipps. See you later.'

He nodded at her, stood up, put on his cap and strode from the saloon. Alone, Carlotta sighed with frustration and drank some coffee. She was sure now that the skipper had instructed Brad to lock her in her cabin last night, and while she appreciated Stan Atkins's concern

regarding the security of the yacht, it annoyed
her when she realised she had been treated not
as the adult woman she was but as if she were a
troublesome, badly behaved adolescent given to
staying out late at night and mixing with the
wrong company. She was convinced now that
the skipper must be acting on orders from her
father.

When she had finished her breakfast Carlotta
left the saloon and went aft to the sun-deck.
There she leaned against the rail and looked
about her. As the skipper had said, the
Montezuma was crossing the bar of the harbour,
rolling a little on the waves that surged across
the long bank of sand and passing two tall ships
anchored just inside the bar. One of them was a
schooner and the other a Hermaphrodite brig.
Carlotta knew they were both charter yachts
that had sailed down from the Virgin Islands.
The brig was making ready to set sail and she
could see members of the crew up in the yards
of its square-rigged foremast, unfurling a heavy
sail.

Once over the bar the *Montezuma* changed
course and turned to port. Its engines picked up
speed as the yacht went south heading for
another island, a series of pointed blue hills on
the horizon.

Moving one of the loungers to face the sun,
Carlotta lay down on it. She smoothed suntan
oil on her arms and legs. She would have liked
to sunbathe without her clothes on, but a certain
consideration for the Atkinses, whom she
suspected of being rather puritanical, prevented
her from doing so. There would be chance

enough for skinny-dipping and sunbathing naked on the beaches of St Phipps.

She lay back and closed her eyes behind the sunglasses. Down in the bowels of the yacht the engines throbbed regularly. The sun was hot and the air soft. She had all the time in the world to relax. There was nothing to bother her except the puzzle about who had actually turned the keys in the doors of her cabin last night.

She was glad they had left Morunda before Phillida Chalmers had come aboard for a visit. Now the embarrassment of having to tell Phillida the truth, admit to the older woman that Kurt was dead and that the man to whom she had been introduced last night was only a deckhand, could be postponed for a few days. She had time to think up some way of avoiding the embarrassment. Perhaps she could say that Kurt had gone away, returned to Europe. No, that wouldn't do because it was possible Phillida might see Brad on the yacht or even in the streets of Morrisburg. But she would think of something. Not right now. Tomorrow. *Mañana*. She smiled a little sadly to herself, thinking of her Spanish-American mother who had never done today what she could put off until tomorrow.

An hour later, alerted by the slowing down of the engines, she left the lounger and went up to the wheelhouse. The yacht was just entering a bay, skirting around some jagged-looking rocks against which water leapt up in fans of spray. Green and gold, covered by giant cacti and feathery-looking trees, two long headlands reached out, seeming to embrace the yacht, gathering it into the almost landlocked bay of

flat, silken water, so clear it was possible to see
fish darting about in the depths.

A hundred yards from the sun-shimmered
beach that rimmed the rocky land at the head of
the bay, the anchor was dropped and the engines
went into reverse. From the wheelhouse Carlotta
watched a deckhand move along the foredeck
below to the bow to check that the electronically
controlled anchor chain was running out freely.
The sun-bleached top strands of his dark hair
glinted and his body, bare to the waist, was
tanned to a ruddy brown. She felt a leap
of excitement as she recognised Brad, her
masquerade husband of the night before.

'That's Stenson Point over there.' Skip Atkins's
voice broke into her confused thoughts, and she
looked round to see him pointing to the green
headland on the right. 'If you look through the
glasses you'll see the stone jetty and a path
going through a plantation of palms. I suppose it
goes to the house. There's the jetty.'

Through the binoculars Carlotta surveyed the
jetty he had indicated, then turned so that she
could see the curve of the beach and the land
rising behind it. Another path was there, twisting
up to a road running along the ridge of land.
Her glance swept on along the road to a gate
and the other headland. Some Jersey cows grazed
the land behind a fence and there was a pen
with wire netting around it where white geese
waddled about. As she studied them a peacock
appeared and showed off its magnificent tail.
With a flutter of white wings, doves swooped up
and then down again.

Changing her stance, Carlotta trained the
binoculars on the only other boat in the bay. It

was a small sailing sloop, and sitting in the
cockpit were a young man and woman and a
blond-haired boy of about two. All were naked.
A faded French tricolour hung from the jackstaff
at the stern of the yacht. She felt sudden envy
of the couple, so contented in their own little
world of their boat with their baby. Then, aware
that she was prying into their privacy, she let
her glance swerve away from them and down to
the foredeck of the *Montezuma*.

Brad was still at the bow, leaning over the
side, checking the anchor, making sure it had
caught. He looked bigger and older than she
remembered, his shoulders very wide, his broad
back shimmering with muscle under his suntanned
skin. As she gazed at him, secretly admiring his
strong athletic body and long sinewy legs, he
moved, turned and looked up at the wheelhouse.
She saw the flash of his teeth as he smiled and
made a signal with one hand to the skipper, a
thumbs-up sign. The anchor was set. The engines
went into neutral and were turned off.

'I think I'll go ashore,' said Carlotta, putting
down the binoculars. She hoped Brad hadn't
noticed her staring at him through them. 'I'll
swim to the beach, take my snorkelling gear. I
won't go for long. I'll come back for lunch and
then later this afternoon someone could take me
over to Stenson Point in the launch.'

'You just please yourself, miss. As long as I
know where you've gone and where you'll be
going while we're anchored here, it's fine with
me.'

Fifteen minutes later, dressed in a sleek green
and white swimsuit, flippers on her feet and
snorkelling mask and tube in place, Carlotta

somersaulted into the clear water of the bay.
Soft and silken, it closed over her head as she
sank downwards. Swimming just below the
surface, she drifted slowly in the direction of the
beach. The bottom of the bay where the yacht
had anchored was covered with grass. She noted
that the anchor was firmly embedded in sand
just beyond the grass. There were no fish, no
coral heads, only smooth banks of golden sand
rippled by sunlight shining through the water.
She stood up. She was in about three feet of
water, and the beach was only a couple of strides
away.

The sun hot on her back and head, she waded
ashore. On the hill above her the geese protested
loudly, honking for all they were worth as they
sensed the presence of a stranger. A few palm
trees shaded the beach. She placed her flippers
and mask behind the trunk of one of them and
walked barefoot up a narrow path to the top of
the ridge. To her surprise the ridge was a narrow
isthmus of land between the Bay of Doves and
another bay on the side of the island that faced
south-east.

Turning, she looked back the way she had
come and felt another jolt of surprise. The beach
where she had come ashore was no longer empty.
A man was there. He was coming out of the
water just where she had waded out, and as she
watched him he sat down on the sand, as
she had done, to remove his flippers. Wide-
shouldered, lean-flanked, his skin the colour of
mahogany, she recognised him easily.

Had he followed her? Probably. Her lips
curled cynically. He probably wanted his US

dollars. Well, he wouldn't get them here. She hadn't brought her cheque book with her.

For a few moments she stood watching him, wondering if he would follow her up the path, but he didn't even look round to see where she was. He lay back on the sand, arms beneath his head.

Oh, well. Carlotta shrugged her shoulders. He hadn't followed her. It was his time off and he'd come ashore to be alone, to sunbathe and sleep perhaps. She turned away, crossed the narrow road that led up to the gate in a barbed-wire fence behind which the geese, the peacocks and a few cattle lived and began to clamber down the rocks to the narrow beach that rimmed the other bay. The geese honked and the peacock shrilled when they heard small stones clanging down the rocks, disturbed by her feet.

At last she reached the firm damp sand against which surf pounded. Exposed to the steady trade wind blowing straight off the Atlantic Ocean, water surged and foamed about numerous rocky islets in the bay.

She lingered at the edge of the beach, tempted to run out into the surf and ride the breakers as they charged in. Then, deciding there would be too many rocks lying beneath the surface for surfing to be any fun, she turned back wondering which was the best way to climb up to the road.

Her heart jumped. Brad was there, sitting among the rocks watching her. He was hardly discernible because he was sitting as still as any rock, his suntanned skin blending with their reddish brown colour, in the shade of a huge cactus.

Perhaps he thought she couldn't see him.

Mischief sparked through her. She would be revenged on him for giving her such a scare. She found a pebble and threw it in best baseball style. It struck a rock just to the right of him, quite close to his face. As she had hoped, it startled him. She saw his head move sharply as he glanced at the rock beside him. Then he looked back at her.

'Hi,' she called to him and waved an arm. 'Come down here. I want to speak to you.'

CHAPTER FOUR

THE man who was sitting so still on the rocks
didn't move right away, and Carlotta wondered
if he was going to ignore her imperious summons.
Then slowly he stood up and began to step over
the rocks. Like her he was barefoot but he
moved more quickly than she had done, leaping
with a catlike grace from one foothold to another,
seeming to know instinctively where to find the
right one.

When he reached the beach and came towards
her Carlotta wished she hadn't asked him to
come down. Naked except for his brief black
swimming shorts, his sun-bronzed skin glowing
in the sunlight, he presented a powerful sexuality
that kept her gaze trapped on him. Conscious
that her heart was beginning to beat much faster
than usual and that her cheeks were unusually
hot, she took in every detail of his muscular
chest and shoulders, the bulge of biceps under
the sleek skin of his upper arms, the strength of
hairy forearms and finally the shapeliness of his
long legs.

He was as lean and graceful as any jungle cat,
yet older than she had guessed him to be the
previous night. By the intermittent light of the
patio, in the silvery radiance of the moon, she
had judged him to be about twenty-nine or

thirty. Now she could see he must be thirty-five, a strong attractive male in his prime.

And just as her glance seemed riveted to his masculine attractions his seemed caught and held by her feminine ones, drifting over her figure, golden-skinned and sleekly curvaceous in the close-fitting swimsuit.

On that crescent of yellow sand, beside the surging green foam-edged water, it was a meeting that vibrated with all kinds of sensual messages, and when he stopped before her, neither of them spoke for a few spellbound seconds. Speech didn't seem necessary.

Then, aware of the sun hot on one shoulder, burning through the oil on her skin, Carlotta stiffened, stepped back a pace and looked out at the bay, away from the mesmerising gaze of his dark eyes.

'I hope you haven't followed me ashore to get the money I owe you. I don't have my cheque book with me,' she murmured.

His eyebrows lifted a little, his lips curled in a slight smile.

'That isn't why I followed you,' he said, also speaking softly as if he had no wish to break the spell.

'Then you do admit you followed me just now, from the yacht?' she said quickly, looking straight at him again.

'Yes, I admit it.' He seemed to become aware that he was standing too close to her, and also stepped back a couple of paces, turning away from her to face the water, shading his eyes with one hand against the glare to look out at some sailing yachts beating past the entrance to the wide-open bay.

'Why? Why did you follow me if not for the money I owe you?' she demanded.

His hand dropped to his side and he turned back to face her again. His lean suntanned face was not easy to read and his dark eyes were shuttered.

'I followed you to keep an eye on you. To see that you don't do anything foolish like drowning or going off with strange men. It seems the last is a bad habit you have,' he said, his voice cool, a little scornful.

'Now just what do you mean by that?' she demanded covering her surprise with a show of haughtiness.

'You eloped with Kurt Malden. And then last night you picked me up in the marina bar.'

'I . . . I didn't pick you up,' she retorted angrily. 'I asked you to dance with me and to help me. But don't think for one minute that because we danced and I asked you to pretend to be my husband you have the right to follow me, or criticise me or to . . . to . . .'

'Take advantage of you?' he suggested smoothly with that annoying satirical flicker of his right eyebrow.

Her breath hissed between her teeth as she drew it in sharply to contain her irritation.

'Please go back to the yacht,' she ordered. 'I don't need your help any more and I don't need you to keep an eye on me. I'll give you a cheque for what I owe you as soon as I get back to the yacht. And that will be the end of it as far as I'm concerned.' She paused, frowning, remembering the number of times she had noticed him hovering near her in the town, in stores, in eating places, in discothèques. Had he been following her then? 'And please stop following me about,' she added.

'You don't owe me anything. Forget that,' he said coldly.

'But you said you wanted to be paid if you pretended to be Kurt. And I'd feel better if I paid you. I'd feel I'm not under an obligation to you for helping me. It . . . it was a wild impulse and . . . and——'

'And now you're regretting it.' He seemed to know how to express what she was feeling better than she did herself. 'I thought you might, and that's why I tried to put you off the idea by asking you how much you were prepared to pay me if I obliged by pretending to be Kurt.' Disgust grated in his voice and his lower lip curled. 'I thought the idea of me pretending to be your husband was crazy, a wild impulse, as you say, that needed to be nipped in the bud.'

'Then why did you say you were Kurt when Bernard asked who in hell you were?' She pounced sharply and felt a vague feeling of triumph when she saw she'd caught him off-guard.

Long fingers raked his hair. He frowned at the distant sailing yachts. The edges of white teeth chewed his lower lip.

'I hadn't reckoned on him being so bloody objectionable,' he growled, 'pushing between us the way he did.' His dark glance flicked back to her. 'But I didn't reckon either on you,' he continued his voice crisping, his face hardening. 'There was no way I could predict you'd introduce me to Mrs Chalmers as Kurt Malden. No way at all. It was you who tipped the fat in the fire. All I could think of to get us both out of an embarrassing situation was to ask Skip Atkins to leave the marina early this morning before Mrs Chalmers turned up and asked to see you and your husband.'

'Hey, wait a minute,' she cried out. 'Did you say *you* asked Skip Atkins to leave port this morning?'

'Yes, I did,' he admitted slowly, frowning again.

'But . . . but you're only a deckhand. You have no authority!' she spluttered. 'Why would Skip do what you ask him to do?'

The dark eyes considered her coolly. She felt as if she were being assessed for qualities she might not possess. The feeling unnerved her. Never had she been surveyed in such a way before. It was like having every defence stripped away and her soul laid bare for his inspection. She couldn't sustain his steady, penetrating gaze and looked away from him abruptly, tilting her chin.

'It's damned hot standing here,' he said at last. 'I wouldn't like either of us to get sunstroke. Supposing we find somewhere in the shade and I'll try to explain everything to you, why I've been following you, and why I have the authority to ask Skip Atkins to leave Morunda this morning. I'd hoped to do what I have to do without you knowing, but again I reckoned without you. I didn't know, you see, that you're given to wild impulses. Nor did I realise . . .' he paused and gave a self-mocking laugh, 'I hate to admit it,' he added, 'but I didn't count on you being so observant or so intelligent.'

Her head swung round. She gaped at him, her eyes opening wide.

'Whatever are you getting at?' she demanded huskily.

'I'll tell you when we're not being fried alive by the sun,' he replied, smiling a little. 'Come on, there should be some sort of shelter from it under the cliffs.'

He turned and began to walk along the beach. In puzzled bewilderment, obeying his order, she followed him. The beach became narrower where the cliffs advanced to the sea. A shallow cave opened up in the rock where the surf had eroded the foot of the cliff.

'How about this?' said Brad. 'Ideal for the purpose of a private conversation while the tide is out. Even some well-arranged rocks for us to sit on.'

Carlotta sat on one of the rocks but he sat on the damp sand. Stretching his long legs before him he leaned back on one elbow, supporting his head on his hand and looked out at the foaming, fretting water of the bay and the shimmering sails of the distant yachts.

'So. Begin. Explain,' ordered Carlotta imperiously, impatient with his silence.

He turned and looked at her, his dark glance raking her.

'Thank God, I'm not really your husband,' he drawled provocatively. 'I'm beginning to think Kurt had one hell of a time with you.'

'I can assure you Kurt gave far worse than he got,' she retorted. 'But we didn't come here to talk about him. What did you hope to do without me knowing or guessing?'

His eyes narrowed, grew wary again as he studied her face.

'To be your bodyguard,' he said quietly.

'My what?' She stared at him. 'But I don't need a bodyguard.'

'Mason J. Burr II,' he began—it seemed to give him some amusement saying her father's full name—'would disagree with you. He hired me to protect you, to go where you go.'

'Protect me from what?' She was indignant.

'From being kidnapped,' he said. His cheek bulged as he probed it with his tongue and the glance he gave from under his eyebrows mocked her. 'Could be he really wanted to prevent you from eloping again with an unsuitable suitor,' he added.

'But why should he think I'd be kidnapped?' she asked ignoring the jibe.

The mockery had gone from his face as if it had never flickered there. The glance he gave her now was serious.

'For some time, since you left Kurt Malden actually, your father has been receiving threatening letters. Anonymous letters. The writer of the letters has threatened to kidnap you and hold you to ransom if Mason J. Burr doesn't go along with his demands.'

'And those demands are?' she queried.

'The letters have been written apparently by someone who feels strongly about the treatment he has received from Burr-Tex oil company and requires recompense. If your father doesn't pay up, the writer threatens to kidnap you.'

'Oh, is that all?' she said with a sigh. 'He's been threatened like that before. People are always threatening to kidnap me, but I never have been, and Dad has never hired a bodyguard before. Why should he have hired one this time?'

'On the advice of his lawyer when he consulted him about the threatening letters,' Brad explained. 'The lawyer suggested that before any steps were taken to search for the writer of the letters someone should be hired to protect you. Since you were going to spend some time on the yacht, your father contacted Skip Atkins and asked him to find someone trained in security who could live on the yacht and keep an eye on you at the same time. Skip contacted me and I flew to Morunda to join the crew just before you arrived.'

'I see.' She was furious, made so by her father's behaviour in doing everything behind her back. 'Dad should have consulted me first,' she seethed. 'This is typical of his high-handed methods. I don't need a bodyguard. I hate being followed about and watched. I'm capable of looking after myself!'

'He doesn't think so, and you can hardly blame him, considering you eloped to marry someone he didn't approve of,' he sneered.

'How do you know he didn't approve of Kurt?' she demanded 'Did he tell you? Oh, I can't believe he would discuss me with . . . with someone he hired, with an employee.' Elbows on her knees she covered her hot cheeks with her hands. 'He had no right to. None at all——' she broke off, unable to express the emotional turmoil caused by the thought that her father could have betrayed her to a stranger.

'It's all right. He didn't discuss it with me. I just guessed,' Brad said softly. 'I didn't even know you'd eloped to marry Kurt until Mrs Chalmers mentioned that your marriage to him was "runaway". I'm sorry. I was out of line for saying what I did just now.'

She flashed a wide-eyed glance at him, encountered a warm, sympathetic expression in the dark eyes before they were veiled by thick, black lashes.

'What Dad didn't understand is that I wouldn't have eloped with Kurt if he hadn't been so critical of him or so over-protective of me,' she said more calmly, responding involuntarily to Brad's warm look. 'Dad's always been suspicious and jealous of any man I've dated. Always. He's presumed all of them to be fortune-hunters.'

'And wasn't Kurt a fortune-hunter?' he queried. He was playing with the sand, lifting a handful of it and letting it slide out through the spaces between his fingers, seeming to have lost interest in her again.

'I didn't think he was when I married him,' she admitted stiffly. 'But I still think Dad should have talked with me before he hired a bodyguard for me. It's time he stopped treating me as if I were a child.'

'Perhaps he would if you stopped behaving like one,' he suggested and the undercurrent of mockery was back in his voice.

'Oh, that's it!' She sprang to her feet. 'I don't have to sit here listening to criticism from you.'

'Sit down.' He was casual no longer. The order was rapped out sharply. 'I haven't finished explaining to you yet. If you stay and listen to me you might learn why your father didn't consult you before hiring me.'

'No. I won't sit down. I'm going right back to the yacht, I'm going to ask Skip Atkins to put through a ship-to-shore phone call to my father

and I'm going to ask Dad to fire you. I don't
want a bodyguard,' she stormed and began to
stride past him.

Her ankle was caught by a big hand. Fingers
of steel curled about its slenderness, threatening
to crush the bones. She lost her balance and fell
across his outstretched legs. All the breath was
knocked out of her. For a few moments she lay
there feeling his knees hard against her breasts.
Then she felt his hand come down on her
buttocks and she tensed all over. But the hand
only slid rather caressingly over her smooth,
rounded rump before being lifted away.

'I'm tempted,' he murmured, laughter shaking
his voice. 'Very tempted. But no doubt you
would sue me for assault or sexual harassment if
I did, so I won't give you what you have
probably never had from Mason J. Burr—and
that is a good spanking.'

Gasping in outrage she thrust the heels of her
palms against the sand and pushed herself away
from him, rolling over to sit up, her legs curled
under her. She was so angry she couldn't speak.
She could only glare at him, her breasts rising
and falling with barely controlled emotion. He
looked back at her and began to laugh, his dark
eyes crinkling at the corners, his teeth flashing
white against the tan of his face, and unexpectedly
his laughter hurt more than the spanking might
have done.

'So what else do you have to explain?' she
demanded haughtily.

He stopped laughing, drew his knees up and
rested his arms on them. Once again his face
was hard, almost grim, and his eyes were
watchful.

'Just this. Your father guessed you would object to having a bodyguard if he consulted you, so we arranged that I should be hired as a deckhand as a cover for my activities.' He paused and looked down at the sand. 'I've followed you about for the past few weeks as unobtrusively as possible. I realise you've noticed me now and again and possibly wondered. It hasn't been easy keeping an eye on you, especially when you've visited a friend, gone into a house or aboard another yacht and I've had to hang around outside waiting for you to reappear. You also have a bad habit of staying out dancing until all hours of the morning. Lately I've been a bit short on sleep.'

'Really?' she found sufficient coolness to mock him in return. 'So why don't you give up? Tell my father you can't keep up with me? I'll be happy to be rid of you.'

His glance dismissed her suggestion scornfully.

'I don't give up,' he replied tautly. 'But this morning when Skip Atkins told me you were suspicious about having been locked in your cabin last night I decided to phone Mason J. Burr and ask his permission to tell you why he had hired me. After warning me you'd probably blow your top when you heard you had a bodyguard he gave me that permission. He knows you pretty well. He knows you're given to wild impulses and have spitfire qualities, contrary moods . . .'

'You're enjoying this, aren't you?' she hissed. 'You're taking a sadistic pleasure in pointing out the flaws in my character. Well, you'd better believe, Mr Bodyguard, that Dad was right. I object very much to having you around watching every move I make, trailing me through the streets of Morrisburg, locking me in my cabin so that you can snatch a few hours' sleep. And now I'm going to phone him, not to ask him to fire you but to tell him I've fired you myself!'

'You'll be wasting your time.' Twisting lithely to his feet at the same time as she stood up, he strode in front of her, blocking her escape from the cave.

Brawny forearms folded across his chest, six feet or more of compact bone and muscle, he towered over her, alert and ready to stop any move she might make to pass him.

'Your father won't fire me on your instructions and I won't leave the yacht or your side if you say you fire me. I was hired by him and I'll be fired by him only. Wherever you go I go until he says stop,' he said with a calm authority.

'You're very sure of yourself,' she countered, tilting her chin at him although she realised she had met her match. There was nothing she could do to get rid of him, at least, nothing she could think of right now.

'Always,' he said. 'I'm glad you've noticed.'

Her glance drifted down from his face over the strong column of his neck, the mat of crisp dark hair on his chest, his flat abdomen and further down to his thighs, straight legs and broad high-arched feet, and once again she felt the tingling pull of sexual attraction. He was different from any other man she had met. Quick-witted, coolly autocratic, he wasn't easily disconcerted and he seemed immune to her attractions, had made no attempt to capitalise on the kiss they had exchanged last night, to take the advantage she had feared he might take. He intrigued her, and she wanted suddenly to know more about him.

'Is your name really Brad?' she asked, looking up at him, with a mercurial change of mood. 'Is it your last name or your first name?'

Only the tell-tale quiver of his right eyebrow indicated that he might have been surprised by her change of attitude.

'It's a shortened version of my last name,' he said curtly.

'Bradley or Bradford or . . .?' She left the question hanging.

'Bradley.'

'And what's your first name?'

'Does it matter?' He was cool. 'You don't have to know. Brad is enough for you.'

'Oh, all right.' She shrugged. 'You're English, aren't you? Which part of England do you come from?'

'London. Does this catechism mean you've decided against phoning your father and asking him to dismiss me?'

'I guess it does.' She smiled at him, her best and most charming smile. 'I like to know something about a person I'm forced to associate with every day. Why did you lock me in my cabin last night?'

'I thought you knew. So I could snatch a few hours' sleep,' he retorted, his eyes glinting. 'To prevent you from going out again. Also to prevent anyone from walking into your cabin at night and kidnapping you. I removed the keys from the doors when I arrived on the yacht and I've locked you in after you've gone to bed ever since you came aboard.'

'Oh.' She had difficulty again in controlling a

quick spurt of anger. 'I wish you wouldn't. I hate being locked in or restrained in any way.' She drew a deep breath to control herself and gave him an up-from-under-look that should have melted his resistance to the appeal she was going to make. 'Now that I know you're my bodyguard and I'm aware of the possibility of being kidnapped will you please stop locking me in? I promise I won't go out at night without letting you know so you can come with me.'

'No.' Her efforts to charm him into relenting had had no effect. He was an immovable object standing there before her, arms folded, iron-hard, impregnable to the assault of feminine wiles. 'I'm still going to lock your doors. You'll get used to being locked in.'

'No, I won't. Never.' Her irritation with him flared out, a flame that should have scorched him but didn't.

'You would prefer to be kidnapped then and held to ransom? You want to put your father through hell worrying about you? Your mother too? Do you have no concern about the people who care about you? Care about what might happen to you?' he accused roughly.

'I don't have a mother. She died when I was sixteen,' she retorted, stung by his remarks. 'And I am concerned about my father. I don't want him to worry unduly about me. It's just that I don't like the idea of having a bodyguard.' Her breast rose and fell as she let out an exasperated sigh. 'Oh, I suppose I'll have to put up with it,' she grumbled sulkily.

'Growing up has always been a painful business,' he jibed. 'We all go through it. Shall we go back to the yacht now? It must be nearly lunchtime.'

'All right,' she agreed. 'But there is something else I ought to mention to you. I'm grateful to you for thinking up a way of us avoiding Phillida Chalmers today, but we've really only postponed the embarrassment of having her come to the marina and asking Skip Atkins if she can see me and my husband when we get back to Morunda. She stays on the island until the end of March.'

'Us? We?' His right eyebrow flickered. His eyes glinted with mockery. 'What's all this? You're talking as if we're partners in the crime of deception!'

'Well, aren't we? You went along with the idea. You didn't have to tell Bernard you were Kurt. You're just as responsible for deceiving him and Phillida as I am,' she retorted.

'That's true,' he conceded. 'I'll think of something during the next day or two while we cruise about the islands to get us out of our masquerade marriage, to divorce us from one another. Don't you worry about it!'

'But you'll tell me, won't you? What you think of?' she said urgently, following him as he walked to the entrance of the cave. 'I'll have to know what you're going to do or even say if we run into Phillida again, so that I don't foul everything up.'

'I'll try to warn you. If there is time and it's necessary,' he replied coolly. 'Now, would you mind if we return to the yacht? I'm ready for my lunch, but until you decide to go back I'll have to stay with you—at a distance, of course, suppressing the pangs of my hunger.' He smiled at her, his eyes dancing with amusement. 'You see how my life is governed by every wild whim of yours. No longer am I my own master.'

His mockery of the situation between them, she as the person who needed protection and he as her protector, struck a chord in her and she laughed, feeling again a strong pull of attraction and they walked along the beach side by side, in a strange but silent communion, as if they knew each other well, as if they were partners, not in crime but in adventure, the adventure of life. As if . . . the thought sidled stealthily and almost unnoticed into Carlotta's mind . . . as if they really were married.

CHAPTER FIVE

ACROSS the road and down the path under the few palms, Carlotta followed Brad to the beach in the Bay of Doves. Under the soles of her bare feet the sand was burning hot and the glare of light on the water was hurtful to the eyes. She searched for and found her flippers and snorkelling mask, and she was just going to join Brad at the edge of the beach, where he was sitting to pull on his flippers, when she heard a high, shrill voice calling her name. Looking round, she saw a woman running towards her, floundering in the soft sand. Behind the woman, drawn up on the beach, was the red Zodiac dinghy she had noticed moored at the jetty below Stenson Point. Suddenly she recognised the running woman and, dropping her snorkelling gear, set off to meet her.

Arms reaching out to each other they met and embraced warmly.

'Tizzy, it's great to see you,' Carlotta exclaimed. 'I was hoping you might be staying at the house. I was going to come over later.'

'It's great to see you, too.' Tizzy was out of breath and her wide grin almost split her thin triangular face in half. As usual her mop of light brown, gold-tipped curls was in an unkempt tangle falling to her shoulders. 'I recognised the

Monte so I went over to see if you or your dad were on board. The captain said you were here on the beach.' She looked past Carlotta, her sparkling grey eyes opening wide. 'Oh, land's sakes,' she breathed in her Texan drawl. 'Who's with you, Carlo? He's super, absolutely super! Trust you to grab the cream of the crop!' Tizzy slapped a hand against her brow as if smitten by a sudden, enlightening thought. 'But of course, you're married now, aren't you?'

Before Carlotta could do or say anything Tizzy launched herself forward, holding out her right hand. Turning, Carlotta saw that Brad had come up behind her.

'Hi,' Tizzy greeted him. 'I'm Teresa Carter and I've known Carlo for years. You must be her husband. What shall I call you?'

'He isn't . . .' Carlotta was beginning when a swift sharp glance from Brad silenced her.

'I'm Kurt Malden,' he said taking Tizzy's hand in his, smiling down at her. 'And what shall I call you?'

'You can call me Tizzy, everyone does. I guess it's because I'm usually in a tizzy about something and right now it's about meeting Carlo and you right here, on this beach!' She gazed up at him and gave a sigh. 'You wouldn't have any brothers, would you?' she went on. 'One between twenty-six and thirty would do. I'm willing to fly over to Europe to meet him.'

'Tizzy, shut up,' snapped Carlotta. The strangest feelings were swirling through her. She didn't like the way Tizzy was hanging on to Brad's hand or the way she was looking up to him. She didn't like the way he was smiling at

Tizzy either and making no attempt to let go of Tizzy's hand. 'You'll embarrass Kurt . . .'

'Sorry, Tizzy. No brothers,' said Brad. To Carlotta's further irritation, he didn't seem at all embarrassed by her friend's brash manner. Then he seemed suddenly to remember he was playing a part, and glanced quickly and enquiringly at Carlotta. Frowning, she shook her head at him, trying to convey that she didn't approve of his behaviour at the same time as letting him know that Kurt hadn't had any brothers.

'That's a pity,' moaned Tizzy, then abruptly abandoned the game of flirting with Brad. Letting go of his hand at last, she turned to Carlotta. 'Ethan's at the house,' she went on, adding for Brad's information, 'he's my brother, and he used to be Carlotta's best beau!

'Tizzy, that was years ago!' Carlotta interrupted sharply. 'It was over long before I went to Europe.'

'It isn't over for Ethan,' asserted Tizzy rather fiercely. 'You'll come up to the house, both of you, to see him, won't you? You see, he can't come to see you, Carlo. Since that plane crash he was in he hasn't been able to walk.'

'Ethan can't walk? I didn't know the accident was that bad,' whispered Carlotta, feeling chilled in spite of the hot sun.

'It's a sort of paralysis caused by a pinched nerve in his spine,' explained Tizzy, serious now, her bright eyes clouded with sadness. 'It's been awful for him, Carlo, but I know he'll cheer up when he knows you're here. Come over now, come for lunch. You too, Kurt.'

'Thank you for the invitation,' Brad said, 'but I would prefer to go back to the yacht for lunch.

Perhaps we could come later, when it's getting cooler.'

'Great.' Tizzy perked up again. 'Come around five for drinks and stay for supper. That OK with you, Carlo?'

'I guess so.' Carlotta couldn't help being truculent. As soon as they got back to the yacht she would have a few plain words with Brad. He was assuming far too much. He was assuming he could decline or accept invitations on her behalf.

'So I'll take you back to the yacht now in the Red Monster,' said Tizzy lightly. 'Come on, Kurt, and help me push off.'

On the deck of the *Montezuma*, after she had climbed up the ladder and Tizzy had zoomed off in the direction of Stenson's Point, Carlotta turned on Brad.

'I don't really want to deceive Tizzy,' she complained. 'I'd have told her you aren't my husband if either of you had given me half a chance. She's been my friend for the longest time and I've never lied to her.'

'How was I to know that?' he retorted coolly. 'I thought you'd had time to explain to her who I was.'

'She . . . she jumped to a conclusion before I could say anything. She knew I'd married and she . . . just assumed you were Kurt. She's like that.'

'Another little rich girl who doesn't think before she acts or speaks,' he jeered nastily. 'Well, the damage is done now, and it might be a good idea to keep up the pretence.'

'But I don't want to,' she stamped one bare foot on the deck. 'I'm going to tell her the truth when I go ashore tonight. I'm going to tell her you're my bodyguard. I'm going to tell Ethan, too.'

His eyes narrowed dangerously and his lips tightened.

'I wish now I'd given you that spanking. Talk about contrary and headstrong,' he said and stepped closer to her, overpowering her with his superior height and heavy muscular shoulders. 'Now, listen to me, princess. We're having no more wild impulses. When we go ashore—I say we because I have to go with you as your bodyguard if not as your pretence husband— you'll say nothing to Tizzy or to Ethan until I give you permission to do so. You'll wait until I've checked out the other people at the house. There could be guests staying with the Carters, people you don't know and have never met before, even your kidnapper could be there. You'll keep your mouth shut and allow Tizzy to introduce us as Carlotta and Kurt Malden. I don't want it broadcast through the social élite of these islands that I'm your bodyguard. The fewer the people who know that the better. Once I've sized up the situation over there I'll let you know if it will be all right to tell your friends the truth. Got it?'

'Supposing I don't get it,' she fumed. 'Supposing I blurt out the truth to Tizzy as soon as we arrive? What will you do?'

'If that's going to be your attitude I'm going right now to tell the skipper to weigh anchor and leave this place because I don't consider it safe for you to be here,' he said grimly and, stepping round her, made for the steps going up to the wheelhouse.

'Oh, no.' She hurried after him. 'No. I don't

want to leave. I want to go ashore. I want to see
Ethan. I promised I'd go. Please, Brad, don't
tell Skip Atkins to leave.'

He turned slowly to face her, eyes still narrow,
his expression hard and unrelenting.

'If you want to see Ethan you'll stay with the
masquerade for a while. If you say one word to
Tizzy or Ethan about our pretence without my
agreement I'll make you look such a fool you'll
be sorry you ever opened your mouth,' he
threatened.

'I hate you,' she flung at him, not able to
think of any other wounding remark.

'Because you can't get the better of me?' he
suggested, 'Or because you're hoping to revive
your old romance with Ethan Carter and that
will be difficult to do with your husband in
attendance?'

'That never entered my mind.' She was wincing
from his jeering jibe. 'I just want to see Ethan,
talk to him. Oh, all right.' She gave in suddenly
as he began to head for the stairs again. 'I won't
say anything to him or to Tizzy until you say I
can.' She tilted her chin at him, and dropped
her eyelashes, trying to achieve a supercilious
pose. 'I'll meet you here around four thirty, and
don't keep me waiting.'

'And between now and then?' he asked.

'Do I have to tell you everything?' she
exploded.

'Just give me some idea of where you'll be.
You must see I have to know where you are to
be able to protect you,' he replied reasonably.

'After a lunch I'll go to my cabin to rest—but
you needn't lock the doors,' she retorted snappily
and went into the saloon.

Carlotta lunched alone on conch salad, a banana and ice-cold lemonade. In her cabin she lolled on her bunk, enjoying the pleasant coolness provided by the yacht's air-conditioning. She tried to read the latest bestseller but found the adventures of the liberated woman who was the heroine of the novel less interesting than her own, so she tossed it aside. Curling up, she closed her eyes hoping to doze as she often did in the heat of the tropical afternoons, instinctively following the habit of *siesta* inherited from her mother.

But, annoyingly, her brain was too active for dozing. It buzzed with all sorts of questions and images. She thought of the threatening letters her father had received and wondered who had sent them. She regretted the lack of communication between herself and her father, which she had increased and widened by her own wayward behaviour. Contrary, headstrong, Brad had called her and he was right, damn him. She was. Or she had been.

Images of Brad crowded into her mind, pushing out thoughts of her father. She saw him as he had been last night, sitting at a table on the patio at the marina. He had attracted her then. Why? Because he had seemed so indifferent to her? She had been the only other person on the patio yet he hadn't glanced at her once, or so she had thought.

The picture changed. She saw him as he had been today, wearing only brief swimming shorts, his suntanned skin glowing, his dark eyes slanting narrow, dangerous glances at her, and her pulses leapt as she felt the tug of his attraction. Better be careful. Once Kurt had attracted her, and look what had happened!

Rolling on to her other side she tried to obliterate Brad with an image of Ethan Carter, but Ethan wouldn't appear. For some reason she had almost forgotten what he looked like. Brad slid before her mind's eye again, dark eyes looking at her now with that hint of sympathy in their depths. As if he cared about her, as if he understood her.

She must stop thinking about him. He was her bodyguard, not her lover, but he was a bodyguard who was her partner in a dangerous deception, pretending to be her husband . . . Her pulses leapt suddenly as she imagined how he might behave if he was really her husband. He would kiss her as he had kissed her last night.

She slipped into a doze imagining she was in Brad's arms being kissed and didn't waken until she heard a knock on the door.

'Come in,' she called, sitting up and swinging her legs over the edge of the bunk.

Jilly entered the cabin carrying a tray set with teacups and a teapot.

'I've just made myself a pot of tea and I thought you might like some,' she said brightly. 'I know it isn't what you Yanks go in for . . .'

'But I'm not a Yankee,' Carlotta interrupted her quickly. 'I'm a Southerner, and I'd love a cup of tea. My grandmother Burr is English, too, and she always has tea in the afternoon, so I'm used to it. Sit down and we'll have a gossip. You can tell me something about Brad.'

Jilly looked up from pouring tea, her grey eyes wary.

'What do you want to know about him?' she asked.

'It's all right. I know why he's with us. He told me when we went ashore why my father has hired him as my bodyguard,' said Carlotta. 'All I want to know is what you know about him. Where and when did you and Skip meet Brad?'

'When we were in the Bahamas, last winter,' replied Jilly. She handed Carlotta a cup of tea with a slice of lemon and took her own cup over to the settee berth on the other side of the cabin from the bunk bed. 'We cruised the Bahamas with your father, your stepmother and your grandmother, so I do know what you're talking about when you say she sticks to her English habits and likes afternoon tea. She's such a sweet lady. She told me she met your grandfather when he was visiting England once. I suppose you have English cousins?'

'Yes. In Berkshire.' Carlotta squeezed lemon into the tea. 'But about Brad,' she prompted.

'Oh, yes. Well, as I was saying, Stan and I met Brad when we were in Nassau. He was living and working there. We brought him on board and he met your father. He told us he was working as a consultant to the Bahamian government, helping to organise a security force to deal with drug-traffickers and terrorists.' Jilly sipped some of her tea. 'He's well qualified to do a security job. He's been with Scotland Yard for years.'

'You mean he's a cop?' exclaimed Carlotta.

'Yes. Or he was. He was in the Yard's D 11 unit for a while. They're a tough lot from all accounts, and are usually called out to guard airports or embassies or government offices when there's been any terrorist threat. He has a desk job now, planning and organising.' Jilly looked suddenly anxious. 'I hope you're not upset, miss, at finding out he's your bodyguard. I'm sure you'll find he's good at it, a real professional.'

'Mmm. I suppose he is,' murmured Carlotta. 'I've never known a cop before.'

'Nor have I,' said Jilly, relaxing again. 'And I wouldn't have guessed Brad was a cop when Stan and I first met him. We were in the casino on Paradise Island, having a flutter at the tables one night and he was right next to us, having his fling too, same as anyone else, betting and losing. He dances well, too. We went to a discothèque with him afterwards and I danced with him. Stan won't dance. Doesn't like rock and roll and that stuff, he says. Is that all you want to know about Brad?'

'Is that all you know?'

'Well, yes, it is really. I can only add that his parents live in Cornwall, his father retired a couple of years ago, and he hasn't been married.' Jilly looked anxious again. 'I hope you're satisfied with him, miss, because Stan and I are right glad your father hired him. We feel less worried about you now that there's someone on board properly trained to keep a look out for would-be muggers or kidnappers. And I'm really glad Brad has told you himself why he's been hired. To tell the truth, I thought it was daft not telling you that he's here to protect you.'

'I guess Dad had good reason for not telling me,' said Carlotta with a touch of irony. 'And yes, I'm satisfied with what you've told me about Brad. I was a bit miffed when I found out why he's been hired but I've calmed down now. He'll be going ashore with me to my friend's house on the island this evening, so neither of us will be wanting dinner, Jilly. We'll come back around eleven, I guess. You might tell Skip.'

'I will,' promised Jilly, getting to her feet. 'Finished your tea?'

'Yes, thanks. It was great. Hit the spot. And thanks again for the information about Brad.'

'You're welcome. I'm sure you'll feel a lot safer with him around,' said Jilly, as she picked up the tray. 'We're all here to do our best for you, miss,' she went on a little diffidently. 'Your father intimated that you'd had a bad time of it lately and that we were to make sure everything went smoothly for you until he's able to join you. I hope you enjoy your visit ashore.'

'I hope so, too,' murmured Carlotta as she pushed open the door so that Jilly could leave.

She spent the next hour choosing the clothes she would go ashore in, showering again and then dressing and doing her hair. Black pants, silky and full, like those worn by eastern belly-dancers. A long tunic created from emerald silk tussore which she clinched at her waist with a gold lamé belt. She wound her hair up into a french pleat at the back of her head and frothed out the shorter strands in front to fall over her brow. With her eyes made up and her full lips red as poppies she thought she looked sultry and seductive. Would she seem like that to Brad, she wondered? And was surprised again by that leap of her pulses at the thought of meeting him and going into the Carter house with him at her elbow posing as her husband.

He was ready and waiting for her at the gate in the yacht's rail. He was wearing another

lightweight white suit, this time with a dark red
shirt open at the neck. After one glance at her,
an all-seeing glance that swept her appearance
from head to toe, he went down the ladder to
the yacht's tender that was bobbing on the water.
She followed him, going down the ladder
backwards and felt his hand take her arm to
steady her when she left the ladder to step down
into the sleek white speedboat.

The sun had begun its swift slide down to the
western horizon and the bay was filled with
golden light. On the Point of Doves the rocks
glowed purple and red and above them the
rough vegetation covering the headland shim-
mered bright green and yellow against the pale
duck-egg blue of the eastern sky. Yet the jetty
that jutted out from Stenson Point lay in the
shadow cast by the bulk of that headland. Tiny
lizards scurried out of the way as Carlotta walked
along the path that twisted up from the jetty
through a plantation of palms, and the heavy
drooping fringes of the leaves rustled and creaked
in the light evening breeze that had sprung up.

Although there was room for them to walk
side by side along the path, Brad walked behind
her which began to irritate her before they had
gone too far. Abruptly she stopped walking and
turned to face him. He was forced to stop too or
collide with her. Jacket pushed back by his arms,
hands thrust into his trouser pockets he looked
at her without expression, his eyes darker than
ever in the shadows. She waited for him to ask
her why she had stopped but he said nothing,
just stood there surveying her with indifference,
she thought, and that annoyed her even more.

'Jilly tells me you used to be a cop with Scotland Yard,' she said curtly.

'I thought you'd be checking up on me,' he replied, the line of his mouth relaxing a little. 'And I'm glad you did. It doesn't do to accept anyone at face value, in your position. It's best to be suspicious of strangers. I'd guess you've never been suspicious of anyone in your life and have trusted everyone.'

'Meaning, I suppose, that I'm naïve and easily taken for a ride,' she retorted icily. 'Another quality I possess that you don't approve of, like my contrariness and impulsiveness.'

'I never said I don't approve of you,' he replied calmly. 'I just pointed out that being the way you are makes it difficult for me—or anyone else—to protect you from harm.' He glanced into the shadows of the trees, then looked back at her. 'So did Jilly satisfy you about my qualification for this job of being your bodyguard?' he asked.

'Oh, Jilly is most impressed by you. She says you must be a tough guy because you were once a member of an élite security team. Do you carry a gun?'

'Sometimes.'

'Now?'

'No.'

'Why not? How will you deal with anyone who tries to kidnap me?'

'There are other ways. Using a gun is a last resort.'

'I see.' With a sudden swing of mood, feeling a sudden and mischievous desire to make him like her, she smiled at him. 'OK, now that I've checked you out and have found out you're a real professional, why don't we walk on together, arm in arm? We are pretending to be married, remember?'

His face froze. He gave her a dark inimical glance.

'Plenty of time for that when we get nearer to the house and might be observed by your friends and their guests,' he said coolly. 'Right now I'd prefer to walk behind you. Then no one can come up on you from behind or from out of the trees without me seeing him or her.'

'Oh.' Chilled as much by his refusal to respond to her smile as by his suggestion that she might be exposed to danger even here on this island, she turned and walked on.

Soon the path gave a final twist and they arrived at stone gateposts. A wide road curved off to the left. Inside the gateposts they followed a driveway between flower beds crammed with blossoming tropical shrubs and shaded by ornamental trees. Ahead of them a whitewashed house with a red-tiled roof glimmered in the fast-falling dusk. A long deck built out from the front of the house and festooned with coloured lights and delicate creeping plants was crowded with people, talking and laughing.

Brad advanced to her side and she felt his hand cup her elbow. A strange shiver compounded of distaste and delight shook her at his touch: dislike because he was a man and touching her, delight because it was Brad touching her.

'Time now for the arm-in-arm bit,' he murmured, letting go of her elbow and lifting her right hand through the crook of his left arm. 'Now we're all set. Do you think we look as if we're married?' Mockery rippled through his voice.

She was unable to respond this time to his mockery in any way. They were fast approaching the wide, shallow steps that led up to the long, covered deck. Tizzy, spotting them, rushed towards them.

'Carlo, so glad you've come!' she exclaimed, and Carlotta, with a new and sharp observation for detail, noticed that Tizzy hardly glanced at her, even though she greeted her hospitably. The gaze of her friend's grey eyes was directed at Brad, and that gaze was boldly admiring, openly flirtatious. Carlotta felt a sort of sickness rising within her. For the first time in all the years she had known Tizzy she felt an unreasonable envy of her, an irritation with her that twitched and niggled somewhere in the region of her stomach.

'Glad you've come too, Kurt,' Tizzy breathed. 'You're *most* welcome.'

Stop it, Tizzy. Stop making eyes at him. Carlotta bit hard into her lower lip so that she wouldn't scream at her friend as Tizzy tucked a hand through the crook of Brad's right arm.

'Come on, Kurt, I'll introduce you to everyone,' Tizzy said. 'Carlotta knows most of the crowd. Ethan is over there, Carlo, by the trellis, in his wheelchair. He's just dying to see you, so go and speak to him right away while I take care of Kurt.'

To Carlotta's secret annoyance Brad's arm dropped away from hers and he went off with Tizzy without a word or a glance. For a moment she stood alone on the edge of the group of guests, feeling deserted and thinking to herself that Brad was a fine bodyguard, going off with her best friend and leaving her exposed to danger.

But she wasn't alone for long. Tizzy's mother, small and blonde, bright as a bird, came up to her.

'Carlo, it's great to see you again.'

Ali Carter's thin arms embraced her and she was kissed on both cheeks.

'Only the other day we were having dinner with Mason and Cora and he was telling us you were down here, staying on the yacht. We were hoping we'd run into you. Tizzy tells me your husband is with you and that he's absolutely gorgeous,' babbled Ali in her scatterbrained way. Then with a glisten of tears in her eyes she whispered. 'Ethan was really badly knocked when he heard you had married. Poor boy. You'll be kind to him, Carlo, please. He's had a lousy time of it lately, with the plane crash and all.'

'Tizzy says he can't walk,' whispered Carlotta, allowing Ali to take her hand and lead her through the guests to a far corner of the deck festooned with blossoming vines.

'He *can* walk,' Ali replied. 'But not very well, and we're having a hell of a time getting him to exercise to strengthen his muscles. I'm warning you, Carlo, he isn't like he used to be. He's lost his zest for life, but I'm hoping the sight of you will recharge his batteries. Now, what's the matter? Who are you looking for?'

Carlotta had stopped, pulled her hand from Ali's grasp and was looking for Brad. He wasn't far away and was being introduced to Caldwell Carter, Tizzy's father.

'I'd like Kurt to meet Ethan,' she said.

'But not right now,' said Ali. 'Later, when you and Ethan have had a little talk.' She took Carlotta's hand again and pulled her forward. 'Hey, Ethan' she called out. 'Look who's here!'

CHAPTER SIX

THE young man of her own age, whose hair was the same ripe wheat colour as her own but whose eyes were a brilliant blue like his mother's, made a supreme effort when she approached him and stood up.

Secretly shocked by his thinness and by the lines suffering had carved in his once-cheerful face, Carlotta dropped her new-found and hard-won reserve, went up to him and flung her arms around him. Tears sprang in her eyes as she realised how badly injured this friend of her childhood and youth had been when he had crashed his light plane. She kissed his cheek and he turned his head quickly to kiss her lips. Then with a little laugh he sat down abruptly in the wheelchair.

'Sorry about that, Carlo,' he said. Reaching forward he caught both her hands in his. 'They give way suddenly. The legs, I mean. Come and sit down. On that chair. Tizzy had it put there specially for you.'

She sat on the edge of the elegant deckchair, her hands still trapped in his.

'Ethan, oh, Ethan, what did you do to yourself?' she whispered.

'I'm not sure what happened. Engine cut out and the plane went into a nose-dive. Next thing

I knew I was in hospital hooked up to all kinds of life-support systems. But what about you? What in hell happened to you? Why did you get married the way you did? We all got the impression the other night your dad wasn't too pleased about your marriage.'

She looked down at their entwined hands rather than face the directness of his blue stare. The urge to tell him that she had made a terrible mistake in marrying Kurt and that her husband was no longer alive was very strong, but she had to contain it until Brad gave her permission to tell her friends the truth.

'I suppose you did it in one of your rebellious moods,' said Ethan. She looked at him. He was watching her closely.

'Guess I did,' she laughed lightly. 'You know me, Ethan. As soon as anyone tells me not to do something I do it. Dad showed his distrust and dislike of Kurt, so of course I immediately wanted to marry him.'

'And now you're regretting it?' he suggested, leaning towards her, his face close to hers.

'Yes, I am,' she admitted and moved back from him a little, but too late, she noticed with a sudden flushing of her cheeks when she looked round. Tizzy was approaching with Brad. They were holding hands.

'Ethan. This is Kurt, Carlo's husband,' Tizzy sang out. Still holding Brad's hand, she looked tiny beside the tall, rugged security man. She was a miniature but very pretty woman, natural-looking with untidy hair and wearing a multi-coloured silk dress. Looking at her friend, Carlotta felt suddenly too tall, too leggy in her baggy pants, too made-up, too much the sultry

seducer, and wished she too had worn a dress
and had tried to look more naturally feminine.
Maybe Brad would have looked at her as he was
looking at Tizzy, with a sort of affectionate
appreciation. Jealousy of Tizzy exploded within
her unexpectedly.

'Glad to meet you, Kurt.' Ethan's greeting of
her counterfeit husband betrayed nothing of his
knowledge that she was regretting her marriage.
He held out his right hand and Brad shook it
and murmured something appropriate.

'We're all going to eat now,' said Tizzy. 'Food
is set out inside. But you two stay here and we'll
bring you some, won't we, Kurt?'

They started to move away. Pulling her hands
out of Ethan's, Carlotta sprang to her feet and
went after them without giving any excuse to
Ethan.

'Kurt, wait,' she said imperiously as she caught
up with Brad and Tizzy at the archway. She saw
Brad's shoulders stiffen and his head go up. He
turned to face her. Shadows from hanging
plants dappled his face, making his expression
unreadable, but she had the impression the gaze
of the dark eyes was cold and hostile. It was
difficult to convey a message to him with Tizzy
hovering at his elbow.

More than irritated with her best friend's
behaviour—it seemed to her that Tizzy was
getting possessive about Brad—Carlotta went
right up to him, smiling at him. She put a hand
on his chest and looked up at him from beneath
her long black lashes and fine, arching eyebrows,
her long fingers playing with a lapel of his jacket.

'Darling,' she murmured, but loud enough for
Tizzy to hear. 'I'd like a word with you.' She

shot a glance at the bright-eyed, inquisitive Tizzy. 'In private,' she added meaningfully.

'But of course.' He played up beautifully. 'Excuse us, Tizzy. I'll come in a few moments to choose food for myself and Carlotta. Now, what is it, sweetheart?' A glint of mockery danced briefly in his eyes and as he lifted her hand from his chest he carried it to his lips and kissed the back of it. Out of the corners of her eyes Carlotta saw Tizzy frown and turn away sharply to go into the house. Immediately Carlotta tried to pull her hand from Brad's grasp but his fingers tightened.

'She's gone,' she whispered. 'You can stop play-acting now.'

'Maybe I'm not acting,' he retorted, smiling at her. 'And there is someone else watching from his corner. Your erstwhile best beau.' He seemed amused by that description of Ethan. 'What is it you want to say to me in private? I guess this is as private as we'll get unless we leave. And you won't want to do that yet. Nor do I. I've seen the food that's spread out inside.'

She did want to leave, she realised. She wanted to give in to the jealous rage that was flaming inside her and drag him away with her, away from Tizzy. She wanted to behave as she would have done if he had really been her husband.

'I . . . I just want to say . . .' She broke off confusedly as the line from Stevie Wonder's hit number jingled through her mind. The next words were *I love you*. She drew a hissing breath. 'To tell you I can't understand your behaviour,' she continued shakily. 'You're suppo-sed to be protecting me. I don't understand how

you can do that if you go off with Tizzy and
leave me on my own . . .'

'But you weren't entirely alone,' he interrupted
smoothly. 'You were with Ethan, quite safe, I
would have thought.' He stepped closer to her.
To anyone watching they must look like a very
loving couple, her hand in his, their heads
touching. 'I've had a good look at everyone
here. I don't think any of them are kidnappers.
They're a well-heeled lot, drawing wealth from
oil companies, I shouldn't wonder.' Dryness
rasped in his voice. 'Not the types to stoop to
criminal activities such as blackmail or kidnapping. Go back now to Ethan and I'll fetch you
some food. I won't be long.'

To her surprise he dropped a light kiss on her
temple and squeezed her hand before releasing
it and, while she was still feeling surprise, he left
her, to saunter, hands in pockets, through an
archway into the house.

'Carlo, come back.' Behind her, Ethan called
to her and turning slowly she went over to him
and sank down on to the chair beside him.
'Judging by appearances only he seems a nice
guy,' he said. 'So why are you regretting having
married him?'

'Mmm?' She was still watching the archway
through which Brad had gone and wondering
just what he was doing in there while he chose
food. Was Tizzy with him, nudging against him,
making up to him, making him laugh? So
engrossed in imagining what they were doing
together, she didn't hear Ethan's question. 'What
did you say?' Dragging her gaze away from the
archway she forced herself to attend to him.

'I said, he seems a nice guy, so why are you

regretting having married him?' The blue eyes regarding her held a puzzled expression.

'Oh, did I say that? What I meant was I'm regretting the way in which we eloped. I didn't realise Dad would be so angry about it. I wish now we'd waited, done it properly,' she said.

'Then there's no chance of you splitting up?' said Ethan looking even more puzzled.

'Splitting up? You mean, is our marriage on the rocks?' she asked.

'Guess I do. You see, Carlo, when he was with us last week, before we flew out here, your dad gave us to understand that . . . well, that you had left Kurt already, and . . .'

'Oh, I had,' she replied a little wildly. 'But he . . . he followed me.' So why hadn't she asked Brad just now if she could confide in Ethan, tell him the truth? Because she hadn't wanted to, because she had wanted to continue with the pretence that he was her husband. She didn't want Tizzy in particular to know the truth. She didn't want Tizzy to feel free to pursue Brad and grab him for herself. She smiled at Ethan, serenely, she hoped. 'We've made it up,' she said. 'We're reconciled. It was only a little tiff, the sort married couples have. Now we're together again . . .' She broke off in amazement at herself. What the hell was she going on like this for? What had happened to the urge to tell Ethan the truth? She decided to change the course of the conversation. 'But what about you, Ethan? Ali was just telling me you won't exercise and won't try to walk. Why not? What's happened to the gutsy guy I used to know? Don't tell me that a little accident with a plane has turned you into a chicken?'

'A little accident?' Ethan began to object, his
eyes flashing angrily. 'If you knew the agony,
the pain——' He broke off and began to laugh.
'Oh, Carlo,' he said. 'You're just what I needed!
How like you to accuse me of lacking guts
instead of soft-soaping me with too much
sympathy. You're right. I have turned into a
chicken, afraid to walk in case walking hurts too
much.' He leaned towards her. 'I wish to hell
you hadn't married Kurt,' he whispered. 'I wish
you'd leave him again or tell him to get lost. I
want you, Carlo. I always have. You're my best
girl. I had it all planned. I was going to ask you
to marry me when you came back from Europe.
But you didn't come back, and I crashed my
plane so I couldn't come after you.'

Carlotta stared at him in silence, trying to
analyse her feelings where he was concerned.
She didn't love him, she knew that, had decided
she didn't before she had gone to Europe. If he
had followed her to Europe and had asked her
to marry him she would have refused him. He
was her friend just as Tizzy was, but she could
never have considered him as a lover.

'I'm sorry, Ethan. I . . . I didn't know you felt
like that about me,' she muttered and with a
sense of relief saw Brad approaching carrying a
tray on which there were plates of food. Behind
him came Tizzy.

But Brad and Tizzy, after bringing food to her
and Ethan, didn't stay to eat with them. They
went back into the house.

'You don't mind lending Kurt to me for a
while, do you?' Tizzy said lightly to Carlotta.
'There's something wrong with the stereo system
and he says he can fix it. We all want to dance

after we've eaten. What's the good of a party if we can't dance?'

Carlotta watched them going wishing she could follow. She did mind lending Brad to Tizzy although she knew she wouldn't have objected to lending Kurt, she thought irritably. What in hell's name was wrong with her? Why get mad just because the guy who had been hired as her bodyguard seem to prefer to be with Tizzy than with her? She had Ethan, didn't she? But she didn't want Ethan. She wanted Brad. The truth seemed to come up out of nowhere and land her a punch in the solar plexus. She gasped. Ethan looked at her sharply and she covered up quickly.

'Hiccups,' she explained. 'I always did eat too quickly. Can I get you more?' She held out a hand for his empty plate.

'I'll come with you,' he said, surprising her, and began to pull himself to his feet. 'Just to show you I'm not chicken!' he said with a grin.

Supporting himself on two aluminium sticks, he walked slowly and with obvious painful effort into the house with her. As they entered the low-ceilinged, wide room where a long table was set with bowls and dishes of food, Ali saw them and came over to them.

'Good,' she said to her son. 'I guess if anyone could get you to move it would be Carlo.' She leaned forward until she could whisper in Carlo's right ear. 'Tizzy is right. He's absolutely gorgeous. Your husband, sweetie. And now I can't understand why Mason doesn't like him.'

'Where is Kurt?' asked Carlotta, frowning as she looked round the room.

'In the den with Tizzy. He's fixing the stereo.' Ali had hardly finished speaking than a number called Columbia Rock blared out through skilfully hidden speakers. 'It seems he's been successful,' said Ali, clapping her hands in delight. 'Oh, he's just the sort of guy a woman likes to have around the house—practical but, oh, so sexy. Now we can all dance!'

But there was no dancing for Carlotta. She sat with Ethan. It was New Year's Eve all over again, she thought forlornly, as she watched the other couples. No one asked her to dance, but this time it was because everyone thought she wanted to sit with Ethan. And Brad didn't ask her to dance because he preferred to sit out with Tizzy, at the other end of the deck.

At last she couldn't bear sitting there watching others dance any longer. Excusing herself to Ethan, she stood up and went to the other end of the deck.

'It's time we went back to the yacht,' she said curtly to Brad.

'Oh, Carlo, not yet,' Tizzy complained. 'Stay a while longer. Stay the night. We've plenty of room.'

'Thanks for the invitation,' said Brad easily. 'But the skipper is expecting us back on the yacht.'

'Then we'll see you both tomorrow. You said you like playing tennis, Kurt. Come early tomorrow morning and we'll play a few sets.'

'No. We can't come.' Carlotta spoke more sharply than she intended. 'We . . . we're leaving in the morning. Going over to St Kitts and then Nevis,' she added quickly. 'It's been good this evening, Tizzy. Great to see Ethan and your folks.' She slid her hand into the crook of Brad's arm. 'Let's go, darling,' she murmured.

He walked behind her again as they walked down the pathway. Fortunately the moon was up and lit the way. When they reached the jetty Carlotta stopped and swung round to face him and as usual spoke what was in her mind.

'Did you have to stay with Tizzy all evening? Did you have to be so attentive to her?'

He didn't reply immediately. Hands in his pockets in typical casual pose he just stood there looking down at her for a few silent seconds. Then he laughed.

'Don't tell me you're jealous of Tizzy just because I like her, because I repaired the stereo for her and enjoyed talking with her?' he said.

'Jealous? Me? Of Tizzy?' She croaked the words out, trying desperately to cover up with a pretence of scornful surprise her startled reaction to his shrewd observation. 'Why should I be?'

'If you're not, why remark on the fact that I stayed with her nearly all evening?' he taunted. 'What did you expect me to do all evening? Sit around and watch you holding hands with your lame boyfriend while he whispered sweet nothings in your ear?'

'Don't tell me you're jealous of him,' she taunted in her turn, although her voice shook a little.

'Yes, I am. As jealous as hell,' he ground the words out and leaned towards her menacingly. Then he seemed to realise what he had said and withdrew, raking a hand through his hair as he turned away from her. He swore rather virulently and muttered, 'This is damned ridiculous. You have no right to be jealous of Tizzy because I stayed talking to her so that you could spend time with Ethan, and I have no right to be

jealous of him because you sat with him.' He
laughed rather drearily. 'You know, we're
behaving as if we're really married.'

'Or as if . . . as if we've fallen in love with
each other,' she whispered.

He turned very slowly and took two long steps
back until he was standing right in front of her
again. Bending towards her he peered into her
face trying to see it by the light of the moon.

'Oh, no,' he murmured. 'I'm not having that.
We've only known each other a bare twenty-
four hours. I admit we're attracted to each other
on a physical level but we're not in love. You're
in love with Ethan and he with you!'

'No. I've never been in love with Ethan. I've
never been in love with any man,' she said
quickly.

'What about Kurt?'

'That . . . that was a foolish infatuation,' she
explained, facing up to the truth about her own
behaviour with Kurt. 'He . . . he led me on to
believe he was something he wasn't. I . . . I
realise now I married him only to spite my
father. I made a mistake and paid for it.' She
paused, then when he remained silent, continued
rather breathlessly, 'And now I know I made
another mistake in asking you to pretend to be
Kurt. They, Tizzy, Ethan and Ali and Caldwell
Carter, all had dinner with my father last week.
He told them about me having left Kurt and
why he disliked him. Now they have met you,
they think you're Kurt. They like you and are
wondering why my father dislikes you. Oh, Brad.
It's such a tangle and I don't know how to undo
it.'

'We could go back to the house now—most of

the guests should have left by now—and tell the Carters the truth, if you like, why we got involved in the pretence in the first place,' he suggested quietly. 'Now that I know no harm can come to you from them I'm willing to let them know I'm your bodyguard and why.'

'I suppose you want to see Tizzy again,' she murmured, feeling jealousy raging through her once more. 'You'd want her to know you're not my husband so you can approach her more openly. You like her more than you like me, and . . .'

'No, I don't like her more than I like you,' he said. Raising his hand, he stroked one finger down her cheek in a casual caress and she quivered from head to foot, not in fear, but because the gentle touch of his finger aroused feelings in her she had never experienced before. 'I like you,' he went on softly. 'I like your golden hair, your golden eyes, your golden skin. You're more beautiful than any woman I've ever been close to before. I like you more than I like Tizzy. I like you but I'm not in love with you. I want you but I'm not in love with you. Do you understand what I'm trying to say, Carlotta?'

'No, I don't.' Emotion was boiling up within her and suddenly it burst through the defences she'd been trying to build up for herself. It overflowed. Putting both hands against his chest she lifted her face to his. 'Hold me,' she whispered. 'Hold me closely like you did last night when we were dancing. I felt safe when you held me. I liked being kissed by you too. Please, Brad, hold me, want me because I want you too.'

He groaned as he put his arms around her.

His cheek brushed against hers. She slid her
hands up over his shoulders and behind his neck.

'Kiss me,' she said, tipping her head back a
little. 'Please kiss me again, like you did last
night.'

Gentle at first, his lips parted hers and the
night revolved around her, moon and stars
spinning. She stroked the nape of his neck and
he gasped with pleasure at her touch, the heat
of his breath entering her mouth in intimate
communion that made her head spin.

They kissed many times, there on the shore
with the moon shining down benignly, long
sense-shaking kisses that obliterated from Carlotta's mind for ever the distaste she had developed
for kissing since her wedding night with Kurt.
She found she couldn't have enough of Brad's
kisses. Her lips clung to his hungrily and she
leaned against him seductively, knowing she was
deliberately arousing hem, feeling the power of
his leashed-in passion in the way his hands
stroked her body through the thin tussore of her
tunic.

But at last he raised his head, seemed to tear
his lips from hers. Breathing heavily he still held
her close to him while he struggled for control.
Against her hair, from which he had pulled the
pins so that it was now rippling down about her
cheeks and over her shoulders, his cheek was
hard, pressing through to her head.

After a while he murmured, 'Was that what
you wanted, poor little rich girl?' His voice
mocked her lightly, belying the passion she could
still feel throbbing through him.

'Yes, and more,' she whispered.

He stepped back from her his hands sliding

PLAY
HARLEQUIN'S

LUCKY HEARTS

GAME

AND YOU COULD GET

★ FREE BOOKS
★ A FREE SURPRISE GIFT
★ AND MUCH MORE!

TURN THE PAGE AND
DEAL YOURSELF IN

PLAY "LUCKY HEARTS" AND YOU COULD GET...

★ Exciting Harlequin Presents® novels—FREE
★ A surprise mystery gift that will delight you—FREE

THEN CONTINUE YOUR LUCKY STREAK WITH A SWEETHEART OF A DEAL

When you return the postcard on the opposite page, we'll send you the books and gift you qualify for, absolutely free! Then, you'll get 8 new Harlequin Presents® novels every month, delivered right to your door months before they're available in stores. If you decide to keep them, you'll pay only $1.99 per book—26¢ less per book than the retail price—and there is no charge for postage and handling. You may return a shipment and cancel at any time.

★ Free Newsletter!

You'll get our free newsletter—an insider's look at our most popular writers and their upcoming novels.

★ Special Extras—Free!

You'll also get additional free gifts from time to time as a token of our appreciation for being a home subscriber.

FREE Mystery Gift
When you return the postpaid card below you could
receive a FREE MYSTERY GIFT! Scratch off the
silver card today!

HARLEQUIN'S

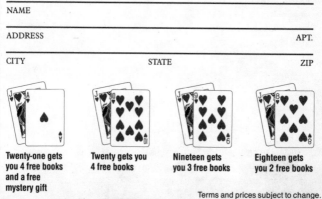

With a coin —
scratch off
the silver card and
check below to see
how many gifts you get.

YES! I have scratched off the silver card. Please send
me all the gifts for which I qualify. I understand I am
under no obligation to purchase any books, as explained
on the opposite page.

108 CIP CAMU

NAME

ADDRESS   APT.

CITY   STATE   ZIP

| **Twenty-one gets you 4 free books and a free mystery gift** | **Twenty gets you 4 free books** | **Nineteen gets you 3 free books** | **Eighteen gets you 2 free books** |

Terms and prices subject to change.
Offer limited to one per household and not valid for present subscribers.

PRINTED IN U.S.A.

HARLEQUIN "NO RISK" GUARANTEE

★ You're not required to buy a single book—ever!
★ You must be completely satisfied or you may return a shipment of books and cancel any time.
★ The free books and gift you receive from this LUCKY HEARTS offer remain yours to keep—in any case.

If offer card is missing, write to:
Harlequin Reader Service®, 901 Fuhrmann Blvd., P.O. Box 1394, Buffalo, NY 14240-1394

BUSINESS REPLY CARD

First Class   Permit No. 717   Buffalo, NY

Postage will be paid by addressee

Harlequin Reader Service
901 Fuhrmann Blvd.
P.O. Box 1394
Buffalo, NY 14240-9963

NO POSTAGE
NECESSARY
IF MAILED
IN THE
UNITED STATES

caressingly down her arms. He lifted both her hands in his, brushed the backs of them with his lips.

'But not now and not here,' he said softly and dropped her hands. 'Lets go back to the yacht before Skip sends a search party to look for us.'

Bemused by his kisses, feeling as if she were walking in a moonlit dream, a dream of a tropical paradise where all her wishes would at last come true, she followed him down to the jetty.

Nothing more was said as the launch zoomed over the flat water, churning up moon-glittered spray. When they reached the yacht Carlotta went up the ladder first and waited on the side-deck for him to join her. Lights glowed softly within the saloon and she wondered if Jilly and Skip were sitting in there.

'I'll tell Skip we've come back,' said Brad crisply turning to her after tying up the launch. 'Shall I tell him also you want to leave here tomorrow morning to go over to St Kitts? Or have you changed your mind and want to go and tell Tizzy and Ethan the truth?'

'I still want to go to St Kitts,' she said. 'Will you be locking me in again, tonight? If so, knock on the cabin door before you do, please.'

'Good night,' he said coolly and walked away from her.

She went down to her cabin. Excitement beat through her as she undressed quickly, put her clothes away and pulled on her nightgown. She removed make-up from her face, brushed her hair, cleaned her teeth.

She had fallen in love again. She knew she had. The knowledge gave her a wonderful feeling

of freedom. She was free at last of the anxiety
she had felt ever since she realised her mistake
in marrying Kurt. She had fallen in love with
Brad and she wanted to make love with him.
She was normal again, no longer fearing close
contact with a man. At least, she didn't fear
close contact with Brad, so she must be in love
with him. Sitting down on the bunk, she swung
her legs up on it, and encircled her knees with
her arms to wait for him to knock on the foor.
She ached inside with desire.

Some time later she lay down on the bunk.
She was trying now to keep her eyes open. She
was also trying to ignore a feeling of deep
disappointment that was mushrooming inside
her, pushing out the earlier joyous feeling of
excited anticipation.

She stared at the cabin door willing it to open
and for Brad to be there, imagining how he
would look at her, his dark eyes lit with the
flames of desire. She imagined how she would
greet him, inviting him in. Surely he would come
soon.

After a while she rolled off the bunk and went
over to the door. She would go to look for him,
following another wild impulse. She grasped the
brass doorknob, turned it and pushed. The door
didn't open. It was locked.

Staring at it incredulously, she backed away
from it, then, whirling, made for the bathroom.
The door in there was locked also. He had come
and locked the doors without her hearing him.
He had come but he hadn't knocked as she had
asked him to. Either he hadn't understood the
message she had tried to convey to him, or he
had deliberately rejected her invitation.

Shaking off a childish desire to yell and stamp her feet in frustration, Carlotta went slowly back to the bunk and lay down again.

So this was what it was like to love and not be loved in return, to desire and not have that desire satisfied. She switched off the light. It was going to be a very, very, long night.

CHAPTER SEVEN

WHITE paint gleaming, windows glittering with reflected sunlight, the *Montezuma* rolled from side to side on the perpetual surge of the small waves. The yacht was moored in the Bay of Basseterre, an anchorage that was wide open to the sea. On the shore the buildings of the town of Basseterre, capital of the island of St Kitts, white and stone-coloured, seemed to dance in a mirage of heat against the hill slopes behind them, which were bright green with sugar cane. High above the slopes the rugged peak of Mount Misery played hide and seek among purple and grey clouds.

It was almost noon, and Carlotta was on the sun-deck leaning on the rail watching for the return of the yacht's launch with Skipper Atkins. The skipper had gone ashore to report to customs and immigration officials, taking with him the yacht's registration papers and the passports of everyone on board. Once he had cleared with the officials and had received their permission to stay in St Kitts for a few days, passengers and crew would be allowed to go ashore if they wished, or the yacht would cruise to a more comfortable, less rolling anchorage in one of the island's more remote and attractive bays.

Carlotta rested her chin in her hands and her

elbows on the rail. She was wearing cream-
coloured bermuda shorts and a sleeveless, multi-
coloured shirt. On her head was a wide-brimmed,
cream-coloured sun hat, and dark glasses screened
her eyes from the bright glare of sunlit water.

She was doing her best to appear at peace
with the world and completely happy with her
lot. She was lucky, she kept reminding herself,
to be there in such a magnificently beautiful
place, on such a luxurious yacht with nothing to
do except sunbathe or swim. Thousands of young
women her age would trade places with her at
the drop of a hat, she mused. They would be
delighted to give up their jobs in offices, factories
or schools or as mothers of tiny tots, just to
have one week in the Caribbean sunshine at that
time of the year.

But right now she would give everything she
possessed just to be one of them, to have a job
to go to, to mix with ordinary people, laugh and
talk and exchange silly secrets with other women,
meet a boyfriend for lunch, go to a movie with
him after work and hold hands in the back row
of the cinema. Being the daughter of a billionaire,
living on a luxury yacht, having nothing to do all
day, wasn't all it was cracked up to be if you
couldn't go where you wanted when you wanted,
or if you couldn't have what you wanted. Being
a rich man's daughter was no fun at all when
you fell in love with a man who told you to your
face that he wasn't in love with you.

She sighed shakily. It was going to be hard
meeting Brad again today and behaving as if
nothing had happened between them last night.
Last night he had kissed her and caressed her as
she had always wanted to be kissed and caressed.

Strong yet gentle, he had aroused in her a desire that could be satisfied in only one way and by only one man—*himself*. By every kiss and every caress, he had shown her too that he wasn't a novice when it came to making love to a woman. He had wanted her, she was sure of that.

Then why hadn't he come to her later? Was it because he was already in love with another woman? Did he have a lover in England who was awaiting his return? Or was the woman he loved and to whom he was committed in Nassau?

'Miss Burr, Miss Burr.' Jilly's voice called her from the wheelhouse. 'Your father is on the phone and wants to speak to you. He's calling from St Thomas.'

'St Thomas?' All her daydreams about herself and Brad scattered to the wind as Carlotta ran up the steps to the wheelhouse. 'What's he doing there?'

'I don't know,' said Jilly. 'He wanted to speak to Stan, but when I told him Stan is ashore he asked to speak to you. He came on the VHF radio. You know how to use it, don't you?'

'Of course.'

In the wheelhouse Carlotta picked up the small microphone speaker that was attached to the VHF radio by a telephone wire. She pressed a button on the side of the microphone and spoke into it.

'Carlotta Burr speaking. Hi, Dad. How are you? Over.' She took her thumb off the button so that she would hear him when he spoke. His voice came through very clearly.

'How are you doing, sugar?' Mason Burr's Texan drawl sounded soft and affectionate, a welcome relief to Carlotta after Jilly's and Stan's nasal whines. 'I'm just waiting around here at St Thomas airport while they fill up the plane's tanks with gas so I thought I'd warn you I'll be landing in Morunda about an hour and a half from now. How about grabbing a taxi and going out to the airport to meet me? Over.'

'You're heading for Morunda?' she gasped, realised she hadn't pressed the button and so he couldn't hear her. She pressed it quickly and started all over again. 'Why are you coming to Morunda?'

'Well, that was the arrangement we made, wasn't it, that I'd join you there just as soon as I could get away? This morning when I woke up I said to Cora that today was the day I could get away and she agreed it was time I headed out to see you. Your grandmother, too. She's been mighty worried about you, honey. Mighty worried. We all have. So, are you going to meet me? Over.'

'We . . . the yacht . . . all of us aren't in Morunda right now,' she stammered. 'We're at Basseterre, in St Kitts. Skip Atkins has just gone ashore to clear with customs. Over.'

'Is that so?' His voice drawled more than ever, something that always happened when he was annoyed and Carlotta tensed as she braced herself for an explosion of wrath. 'Well, you can just tell him from me when he returns to the yacht to turn around and go right back to the customs house to get permission to leave. Got that, honey? Over.'

'Yes. But . . .' She paused, realising the futility of arguing with her father. When he issued orders you obeyed him. 'Are you piloting the plane yourself?' she asked, guessing he had flown from Dallas in a series of short hops.

'Sure thing. But Candy is with me.' Candy was the young Mexican he employed to look after the plane and to pilot it when he couldn't. 'Tell Stan I expect the *Monte* to be back in her berth before sunset this evening. I'll be on the dock to catch the lines. It shouldn't take you more than four hours from Basseterre to Morunda. OK? Over.'

'Yes, OK. Take care, Dad. Over and out.'

'You take care, too, sugar. Over and out.'

Carlotta spoke into the microphone again, giving the yacht's call sign and name, said she was returning to the stand-by frequency channel, pressed stand-by numbers on the radio followed by the enter button, then hung up the microphone. Immediately a voice came through calling another yacht in the vicinity. She turned down the volume and turned to Jilly who had returned to the wheelhouse.

'Dad is flying to Morunda. He'll be there in an hour and a half. He wants us to be back at Brock's by sunset today,' she said.

'Oh, bother,' said Jilly mildly. 'Stan won't be at all pleased. He'll have to go straight back to customs to clear us before we can leave.'

'I know. Perhaps we could catch him before he leaves the customs house,' suggested Carlotta. 'We can call them on the VHF, can't we?'

'We can try.' Jilly sounded doubtful. 'We'd have to call the police control and pass the message through them. Anyway, Stan has possibly left customs by now and gone to the market for me.'

'Then our best bet is to send someone ashore

in the other dinghy, to tell him what's happened before he comes back to the boat. How about sending Willy in the Avon dinghy?' suggested Carlotta.

'Willy has already gone ashore with Stan. To visit his family who live in the town.'

'Then I'll go,' said Carlotta. 'It will give me something to do and I'd like to see something of the town, anyway, before we have to leave.'

'Why don't I just ask Brad to go over?' Jilly said. 'If you go, he'll have to go with you anyway.'

'But I want to go,' asserted Carlotta. 'I don't want to have to leave St Kitts without having seen something of it. Go and tell Brad to launch the dinghy and I'll be with him in a few minutes.' She listened to herself giving orders just like her father did with a little flicker of surprise. She had never considered herself autocratic before. 'I just have to pick up my shopping bag and purse from the cabin.'

Before Jilly could present any arguments Carlotta skipped out of the wheelhouse and down the steps to the sun-deck and then to her cabin. Ten minutes later, little sparks of excitement chasing through her at the thought of meeting Brad again, she went up to the main-deck and along to the gate in the rail. The Avon dinghy had been launched and was bobbing on the waves at the ladder, and Brad was standing by the open gate keeping an eye on the dinghy while listening to Jilly who was giving him instructions.

'Good morning, Brad,' said Carlotta, breezily for Jilly's benefit.

'Good morning, miss.' Dark glasses covered

his eyes so it was impossible to see the expression in them. Below the glasses his clean-shaven jaw was taut, his lips unsmiling.

'I was just telling Brad where the only supermarket in the town is located,' Jilly explained. 'If you don't meet Stan returning to the pier you'll find him near the market or on his way back from it. I don't think you'll miss him.'

'I hope we won't,' said Carlotta and made for the gate to go down the ladder. 'I'll drive, Brad,' she said brightly.

Seated in the stern of the little dinghy, she soon had the outboard engine going. Painter in hand, Brad joined her and sat in the bow of the boat, his back to her. The noise of the engine made speech impossible unless they yelled at each other.

From wave to wave the dinghy bounced, sending up showers of glittering spray. Carlotta went at full speed, although she knew from past experience of having sat in the bow of this particular dinghy that the person in the bow would be getting wet. It gave her a certain mischievous pleasure to know that Brad was getting soaked. It was her small revenge on him for having rejected her last night, she thought.

She half-expected him to turn and ask her to go more slowly, or even to move from the bow to the centre thwart. But he didn't turn or move. He just sat there stoically, putting up with the discomfort rather than look at her or speak to her. Stoicism, she guessed, was an important part of his character. Tough, disciplined, stoical. He was all of those, so how could she, naïve and inexperienced as she was, hope to plumb the depths of the passion which she knew now boiled beneath his outer control? How could she rouse him to the point where he would consider the world well lost for the sake of a passionate affair with his employer's daughter?

The pilings of the old pier loomed up, green with slime. Obeying a sign from Brad as he pointed to the left, she steered the dinghy past the end of the pier to the leeward side where there was a floating dock. The yacht's launch was tied up there.

On the pier a row of youths, brown faces shining, white teeth grinning, looked down at Carlotta and Brad as she steered the dinghy to the dock. All of them shouted encouragement to her and two of them leapt down from the pier to the dock. They approached the dinghy, holding out their hands. Both of them were very skinny and were dressed in frayed, cut-off-jeans shorts and ragged T-shirts. Their feet were bare.

'I saw you first, sir. Lemme take your rope and tie it up. Lemme be your guide,' said the bigger of the two.

'I'm Isaac, sir. You won't find no better guide than me in all of St Kitts. Take no notice of him, sir. He's a commie and not to be trusted!'

'Hey, that's not true.' The bigger youth punched at the smaller one who staggered backwards and, realising he was near the edge of the float jumped into the water. The bigger one, losing his balance, also fell into the water. While they were spluttering and laughing, Brad sprang ashore, tied the dinghy painter to one of the pilings of the pier and turned to help Carlotta, holding out a hand to her.

She decided to be independent and with the

handle of her big canvas shopping bag over one shoulder, sprang ashore just as he had and made for the broken ladder that led up from the float to the top of the pier. As she reached the top of the ladder the rest of the youths, the four who hadn't jumped down on to the float, crowded around her, all of them offering to guide her to the town, buy ice for her, get gas for her if she paid them a few dollars. Laughingly, she told them she didn't want a guide, but they still hopped around her as she walked towards an open gateway in a steel fence that protected a long yard behind a warehouse building. Then suddenly they were all gone, scampering back to the pier, driven away by sharp authoritative words from Brad.

Across the yard and into an alleyway between the warehouse and the next building, high, old-fashioned and painted a bright turquoise. It was the customs building and the doors were closed. A notice stated that the office closed at noon and re-opened at one o'clock. Carlotta looked at her watch. The time was ten minutes past twelve.

'He must be at the supermarket or coming back from there,' she said. 'But as it is he'll have to wait until one before he can get clearance for us to leave.' She glanced up at the impassive face of the man who was standing beside her. 'Did Jilly tell you my father is on his way to Morunda and expects us to be at the marina by sunset today?'

'She did.' Cool, indifferent, he didn't look at her.

'What are we going to do now?' she whispered.

'Find Skip Atkins and be in Morunda by

sunset, I suppose.' He shrugged his shoulders as if the matter didn't concern him.

'I don't mean that and you know I don't. I mean what are you and I going to do about our pretence?'

'Hope that he doesn't find out?' he suggested, shrugging again.

'But if he does?' she persisted.

'Then you'll just have to tell him why you needed an instant husband and hope he'll understand,' he replied coldly.

'Implying that you had nothing to do with it, I suppose,' she retorted, suddenly irritated by his indifference. 'Yet if you hadn't gone along with the idea in the first place and hadn't introduced yourself as Kurt to Bernard, if you hadn't let Tizzy think you were Kurt, there wouldn't have been any pretence.'

'OK.' His voice drawled wearily and he shrugged again. 'Tell him it was my idea if you like. Put the blame on me and he can fire me. I've had enough already of this job of being your bodyguard. It's getting to be boring.'

It was like being stabbed to the heart. She turned to him, only vaguely aware of the noises of the street, the people walking by, cars hooting at each other, the deep shadow on one side, the bright sunlight on the other. His arms folded over his chest, he was standing at ease with his legs apart and he wasn't looking at her.

He was staring back along the street the way they had come, presumably looking for Skipper Atkins.

'That wasn't fair,' she muttered. She couldn't think of anything else to say to express the pain she felt at his wounding remarks.

The dark glasses glinted as he glanced down
at her and the rebellious lock of gold-streaked
straight dark hair slid forward on to his forehead,
but there was no softening of the line of his lips
and it seemed to her that his jaw was cast in
bronze.

'Love and war seldom are fair,' he retorted
coolly. 'Shall we go on now, towards the market?
I don't want to miss Skip.'

A hand under her elbow he turned her round
and they walked along the narrow street until it
widened out into a sort of promenade beside the
bay. Palm trees rustled and swayed in the wind
blowing off the sea and groups of young men
who were walking about shouted to each other.
They hadn't gone far when they saw Skip coming
towards them, carrying a shopping bag. He was
surprised to see them, but grateful when Carlotta
explained why they had come.

'Not that I can do much about it now,' he
said, as they dawdled back towards the post
office. 'I'll have to wait until customs open up
again at one. Then they're so slow and meticulous
about everything. We'll be lucky if we're able to
weigh anchor by two and even luckier if we
reach Morunda before sunset.'

'Just as long as we get there today,' said
Carlotta consolingly. 'Shall we go and have lunch
somewhere while we wait for customs to open?
Or is there time for us to take a taxi to
Brimstone Hill and visit the fort?'

'I doubt we could get to Brimstone, see the
fort and be back here before two,' replied Skip.
He lifted his cap and wiped sweat from his
forehead on the short sleeve of his shirt. 'Lunch
sounds good to me. Wouldn't mind a couple of

ice-cold beers. There's a good hotel-restaurant in the Circus. We could sit on the balcony and watch the locals.'

The Circus was so called because it was an oval-shaped space planted with tall palms, with a Victorian-styled clock tower and drinking fountain in the centre. Cars were parked all around the edges of the Circus, and at lunchtime it was full of men, some in smart, tropical, lightweight suits and some in jeans or shorts and T-shirts, eating their lunches from brown paper bags or just lounging about exchanging jokes and gossip. The whole area vibrated with vitality and noise.

'It's a pity we have to go back to Morunda before you've seen much of this island,' said Skipper Atkins. 'It's not a state-of-the-art, tourist-dominated island like Morunda, thank God, although there are excellent hotels where you can stay and fine beaches to swim from.'

'How did it get its name?' asked Carlotta. Brad was silent, almost sullen, she thought, making no effort to join in conversation.

'From Christopher Columbus. He discovered it on his second voyage to the islands,' explained the skipper. 'But the first settlers were English. They established the first British town up the coast at Roadtown. Then the French came and settled here, in Basseterre. British and French lived together fairly amicably until 1666 when all hell broke loose. That was when the British started to fortify Brimstone Hill to protect their settlement. When we leave we'll run up the west coast and you'll see the fort. You could photograph it from the yacht if you have the right lens.'

Carlotta was glad Stan Atkins was a chatterbox

and that his knowledge of the island was intimate, and with the right few words she encouraged him to go on with his potted version of the history of the island.

'When did the French leave?' she asked.

'They said they'd left for ever in 1713,' he returned drily. 'But they were back in the 1780s and forced the British to surrender. They withdrew later and the British regained control. The French returned in 1805 and proceeded to hold this town to ransom. Since then the British had it to themselves until the island received its independence a few years back.' Skip paused, took a deep drink of his second beer and added, 'Talking of ransoms, I take it you've had no trouble keeping an eye on Miss Burr these past few weeks, Brad. No one has tried to grab her?'

'It all depends on what you call trouble,' Brad said slowly, one eyebrow flickering. 'My problem is I never know what she's going to do next!'

Across the table she glared at him, then realised he couldn't see the expression in her eyes because of the sunglasses. If she could have kicked his shin under the table she would have done.

'You must keep him informed, Miss.' Skip Atkins was deadly serious and she experienced a hysterical desire to laugh at the irony of the situation. 'Of where you're going, I mean. And make it possible for him to go with you.'

'I do and I have,' said Carlotta sweetly. 'But I can't help it if Brad allows himself to be distracted by other people when I go visiting. Last night he was far more interested in entertaining my friend Tizzy than he was in protecting me.'

The feline in her knew a certain gloating triumph as she saw Brad's face colour, red running up beneath his tan, and she guessed that if she could have seen the expression in his eyes she would have fallen dead on the spot. She smiled sweetly at him. He scowled and looked away.

Skip Atkins, as if sensing that his two companions were on the verge of war, cleared his throat uncomfortably, finished his beer at a gulp and rose to his feet.

'It's five past one and I'd like to get over to the customs office now,' he said. 'There's just one problem: Willy. He's visiting his mother here in town. I told him to take his time because we wouldn't be leaving until about five to cruise down to Frigate Bay to spend the night there. Someone will have to go and fetch him.'

'Tell me where he is and I'll go and get him,' offered Brad obligingly, also standing up. 'That is, if you think you can keep Miss Burr in order. A visit to customs with you might improve her education. I don't suppose she has much idea of the patience and sheer persistence required to be skipper of a private yacht.'

Suppressing a wilful urge to stick her tongue out at him, Carlotta stood up too.

'I'll be only too pleased to stay with you, Skipper,' she said. 'And to go back in the launch with you. Brad and Willy can return to the yacht in the Avon.'

Outside the hotel, in the noisy, sunny Circus, the skipper gave Brad instructions about where he would find Willy and Brad strode away along a street that went uphill from the Circus. He left her and the skipper as if glad to go, thought

Carlotta as she crossed the Circus with Stan Atkins, glad to be rid of the responsibility of protecting her, if only for a short time.

Yet last night he had told her she was beautiful. Last night he had told her he liked her. Last night he had kissed her as if he had wanted her.

Puzzling over his cold and almost cruel treatment of her that morning and during lunch, she entered the customs building with the skipper. It was a relief to get into the cool, spacious, if shabby, hallway of the old Victorian building and escape from the midday heat. Inside the skipper paused to take off his cap and to wipe sweat from his face and neck while she held his shopping bag. After stuffing his handkerchief into his shorts pocket he gave her a worried glance.

'I'm sorry you're displeased with Brad,' he said rather stiffly. 'But if you're not satisfied with his behaviour you must tell the boss when you see him tonight.' He turned his cap between his hands and stared at it as if it were to blame somehow for his anxiety. 'I didn't think Brad would ever step out of line,' he muttered. 'I suppose I assumed he would do a right good job, be a real professional, when your father asked me for my opinion of him. I recommended him and now I feel responsible for his behaviour . . .'

'But you mustn't feel like that,' Carlotta interposed quickly, cursing herself for her mischievous tongue. 'Brad has done a great job. Really.'

'But you said he paid more attention to your friend last night than to protecting you, and you know as well as I do, Miss, that a hired bodyguard isn't supposed to spend his time socialising with your friends. If you don't tell the boss I'll have to.'

'No, oh, no. You mustn't do that.' Carlotta's voice echoed in the high empty hallway. 'I . . . I was only teasing Brad, at lunchtime. Please don't you say anything to my father. I'll tell him, explain everything. It will be all right, I promise you.'

He didn't look convinced, but he didn't persist, and, turning away, began to mount a wide stairway to the next floor. Carlotta followed him, thoughtfully.

CHAPTER EIGHT

LIKE a luxurious emerald-green tent the island rose up out of the sea. The lower slopes of the hills were bathed in golden afternoon sunlight while white and purple clouds capped the craggy peaks of its three mountains. From the sun-deck of the *Montezuma*, which had left the rolling anchorage of Basseterre at exactly two o clock, Carlotta surveyed the shore of the island through the telephoto lens of her camera. Beside her Skip Atkins did the same. He had left Jilly in the wheelhouse to supervise the automatic pilot as the yacht ploughed through the white-crested waves along the western coast of St Kitts.

Even after they had passed the distinctive and spectacular Brimstone Hill, an upthrusting mound of rock surrounded with stone fortifications built by the British and flat green fields close to the shore, Carlotta stayed on the sun-deck watching the rest of the island slide by, forgoing her afternoon *siesta* and listening to Skip Atkins talk about the history of the island, about photography, about anything that came into his head. He was, it seemed to Carlotta, paying her a lot of fussy attention, far more than he usually did and she wondered if—to use a phrase of her English grandmother—he was buttering her up for some reason.

When the yacht reached the north-west point of St Kitts the skipper left her to return to the wheelhouse to supervise a change of course and Jilly came down to join Carlotta, to chatter cheerfully of this and that, increasing Carlotta's suspicion that the skipper and his wife were worried about what she was going to say to her father when she met him in Morunda.

The bow of the yacht turned to the right, to starboard, and they entered the wide channel between the north end of St Kitts and the Dutch island of St Eustatius, called locally Statia. Its volcanic peak half-hidden under a puffy white cloud, the small island looked like a flattened Dutchman's cap made from green and yellow felt.

Called back to the wheelhouse by the skipper, Jilly left the sun-deck and, alone, Carlotta saw the hills of Morunda appear on the horizon as the yacht surged out of the channel and into the open sea again. The weather was changing. As often happened between three and five in the afternoon the trade wind was increasing in strength. Fast-moving clouds frolicked across the sea from the south-east. The water was darkened by their shadows and churned up by the strengthening wind.

Slanting rain hit the yacht. Carlotta ran for shelter into the saloon. The yacht rolled and lurched under the onslaught of the sudden squall. Jilly appeared through the other entrance to the saloon.

'Are you all right, miss?'

'Sure I am,' said Carlotta. 'Do you know where Brad might be?'

'In his cabin. He said he was going to catch

up on his sleep this afternoon since there was nothing much for him to do?' Jilly gave her a curious yet wary glance. 'Skip has been telling me you're not too happy with Brad's behaviour....'

'Oh, no, no. I told Skip not to worry about what I said to Brad.' Her suspicions had been right then. Skip and Jilly were worried about what she might say to her father, not so much about them but about Brad. 'I was only teasing Brad at lunchtime. I'm not going to complain about him to Dad,' she added, irritated with herself because she been so outspoken in front of Skip Atkins.

'You might tell him that, then.' Jilly was still looking anxious.

'I will. Which is his cabin?'

'Number four in the fo'c'sle,' Jilly replied without hesitation, her face resuming its usual expression of cheeriness. 'But I expect he'll be up on deck before we reach Morunda. You could say something to him then, just to relieve his mind. I think he believes you're going to have him sacked, miss.'

'All right. I'll see him, then. I'll just go and put my camera away now. The squall seems to have passed through.'

But although the rain had stopped, the clouds had rolled on and the sun was shining again, the yacht was still lurching about on the bigger waves and Carlotta had to hang on to the rail of the companionway as she made her way down to the lower deck. In her cabin, she stowed her camera carefully in the bag where she kept all her photographic equipmentand put the bag in the locker. She had learned the hard way when she had first cruised on the yacht not to leave anything valuable or breakable lying about carelessly. In a sudden squall like the one they had just had anything could go flying across a cabin and break if it hadn't been chocked off and prevented from sliding about a shelf.

Her camera put away, she lay down on the bunk thinking she, like Brad, might also catch up on her sleep. What a nuisance she must seem to Skip and Jilly, she thought, with her impulsive behaviour and her way of speaking without thinking. She had never considered before how responsible they might feel for her well-being. Nor had she ever thought how dependent they were on her good opinion of them. Their jobs, she realised with another flicker of irritation at herself, depended on her giving a good report of them to her father.

How would her father react when he learned of her latest escapade? She would have to tell him that she had asked Brad to pretend to be her husband before he ran into Phillida or Bernard. He might be angry with her but he would be more so with Brad. He might sack Brad on the spot and then sack Skip and Jilly for having recommended Brad.

As for Brad, what was he thinking now about her? Cold and sardonic this morning, he had said he had found being her bodyguard boring. With a few calculated and cruel remarks he had set her at a distance, and now he must be thinking that his own opinion of her was right. She was a person who never thought.

An urge to go and find him and to explain she had been only teasing him about Tizzy at lunchtime was very strong. She didn't want to wait until he was on deck and preparing for the

docking of the yacht at the marina on Morunda.
She wanted to talk to him now, to cross the
distance he had made between himself and her,
to get close to him again.

Yet the urge bothered her. Was it just another
wild whim, an impulse she would regret later?

Slowly she rolled off the bunk and went over
to the door. She opened it and looked out into
the passageway. Save for the humming of the
engines and the swishing of the sea against the
hull, all was quiet. Slowly, she stepped over the
high sill and closed the cabin door. For just a
moment she hesitated, before making her way
forward along the central passage to the door
that separated the crew's quarters in the fo'c'sle
from the owner's and guest cabins in the after
part of the yacht.

Cabin number four was the first she came to
after stepping into the fo'c'sle. Again she
hesitated before knocking on the door, her
cheeks flushing red at her own effrontery in
actually coming this far. Never before in her life
had she pursued a man. Always she had been
the pursued not the pursuer. And never had she
intruded on anyone's privacy before. She prized
her own privacy too much ever to have done
that.

But the urge to see Brad and to talk to him
was fast developing into a raging torrent that
was sweeping all puritan reserve before it. She
raised her fist and knocked sharply on the door.

Nothing happened, and in a down-swirl of
anticlimax she turned the doorknob and pulled
the door open, fully expecting to see an empty
cabin and drawing a sharp breath of surprise
when she saw Brad lying on the bottom one of

two bunks, his back to the door. He was dressed only in the white uniform shorts and the skin of his long wide back shone, smooth as reddish-brown silk, tempting her hands.

The cabin was much smaller than hers, only about six feet wide, and when she stepped in and closed the door after her she found she was standing very close to him, close enough to be tempted even more to slide her fingers over his shoulders, to ruffle his already tousled hair, to bend close to him and whisper in his ear.

Instead, hands clenched at her side, she stood still and upright, her feet apart as she adjusted her balance to the lift and roll of the yacht and said loudly, 'Brad. Wake up. I must talk to you.'

Muscle rippled beneath smooth skin as he stiffened. For a moment he lay still yet alert. Then he moved, turning and sitting up all in one movement, raking back his hair. She saw his face harden and his eyes narrow to slits.

'What the hell are you doing in here?' he demanded. 'Get out.'

As she had guessed, he was angry with her for having intruded and, hurt by his reaction, she almost turned and fled. But the magnetism between them had begun its subtle action. It seemed to glue her feet to the spot, her gaze to his upturned face.

'I knocked but you didn't answer,' she explained haltingly. 'I . . . I only opened the door to look in to see if you were here . . .'

'I was dozing,' he cut in coldly. 'You didn't have to come in. Looking in would have been enough. Now, go away.'

'But I must talk to you,' she argued.

'Then give me a couple of minutes to put on a shirt and I'll come up to the saloon,' he replied crisply. 'Go on, get out. There's hardly room for me in this cabin, never mind you as well. I can't put on a shirt with you in here.'

'You don't have to put on a shirt,' she said. The boat gave a bigger lurch than usual and she lost her balance and, turning quickly, sat down on the edge of the bunk beside him. 'I can say what I have to say here. No one will interrupt us or overhear us.'

'I would rather hear what you have to say in the saloon.' He inched away from her along the bunk, his expression hostile. Suddenly he swore, a crisp crashing oath uttered between taut lips and she flinched. 'Why did you have to come in here?' he demanded in a goaded voice. 'The one place where I can escape from you?'

That hurt more than anything else he had said to her. She stiffened, hiding her hurt as always beneath a pose of hauteur.

'It won't take long. I just wanted you to know I'm sorry about what I said at lunch,' she said in flat, controlled voice, not looking at him but at the opposite wall of the cabin covered with built-in lockers. 'About you and Tizzy. I only said it to get back at you for some of the nasty remarks you'd made to me,' she continued. 'And I realise now that it upset Skip Atkins. He and Jilly think I'm going to complain to my father about you and about them for recommending you. But it's all right. I won't be complaining about you or them and I won't be blaming you for the pretence. I know you wouldn't have pretended to be Kurt

if I hadn't asked you. I know I'm to blame for
what happened.'

She paused. He didn't speak. The silence
was laden with tension and the atmosphere in
the small cabin was stifling. Outside the few
inches of thick fibreglass and insulation that
separated them from the sea, water swished
and sprayed against the hull as the yacht surged
forward.

'But I'll have to tell Dad about it. I'll have
to tell him before Phillida or Bernard or anyone
else tells him they know Kurt is with me,'
Carlotta muttered, looking down at her hands
which were gripping each other nervously on
her knee. 'You do see that, don't you?'

'Yes, I see it.' He spoke coldly. 'But I've
already told you I don't care if he does decide
to give me the sack.'

'Oh, but I do.' She turned to him, her
control swamped by a flood of emotion.

'Well, well, this is quite a change from
yesterday morning,' he jeered. 'Yesterday you
were all set to phone him to ask him to fire
me. Carlo, Carlo, quite contrary!'

'Oh, stop it, stop it!' She clapped her hands
over her ears. 'Stop making fun of me.'

The mockery faded from his face. It became
as blank and hard as a statue's.

'Then get out of here,' he said clearly and
loudly so that she could hear him through her
hands.

'Not yet.' She dropped her hands on to her
lap again. Pride dictated that she should leave
when he had made it so clear he didn't want
her in his cabin, but she still had something to
say. 'I know I must seem contrary,' she said,

not looking at his face but at his powerful thigh, so close to hers. If she reached out one hand she could touch it, stroke the bare skin, feel the muscle and sinews tauten beneath her fingers. The need to touch him, to let magnetism have its way, was causing her to ache inside. Her hands clenched again and she looked away, down at the floor of oak strips. 'But, then, so much has happened since yesterday morning,' she added with a sigh.

'Has it? I hadn't noticed.' Abrupt, acidic, his remark seared her, but she refused to be deterred by his jeers. Swallowing hard, sinking her pride, she raised her head and looked directly at him. He looked back at her, his dark eyes wary as he leaned away from her, resting his back against the wall at the head of the bunk.

'I waited for you last night,' she said as steadily as she could. 'I hoped that when you came to lock the doors of my cabin you would knock first. Why didn't you?'

'I decided that discretion was the better part of valour,' he replied coolly.

'So what's that supposed to mean?' she demanded sharply. Was there no way she could get through his steely defences? 'Don't talk to me in riddles. Give it to me straight in basic English.'

His eyes widened a little, but his expression was still hard.

'All right, you asked for it,' he said harshly. 'This is as straight and as basic as I can get. I decided not to betray Mason J. Burr's trust in me by laying his daughter.'

Carlotta flinched. She couldn't help it even

though she guessed he was deliberately trying to antagonise her by reducing what might have happened in her cabin the previous night to its lowest and, for her, most insulting terms.

'That was insulting.' she whispered.

'It was meant to be. Your father hired me to protect you, not to sleep with you. You've said what you came here to say, so get out of here. Go.' Hard and cold as bullets his words hit her but she didn't move.

'Why? Why are you trying to hurt me?' she asked shakily. 'Last night you told me you like me and you kissed me and touched me as if you wanted me. It seems to me your feelings are as contrary as mine, blowing hot then cold.' She leaned towards him suddenly, trapping him. He drew a sharp breath and closed his eyes. 'Brad, be honest with me,' she pleaded. 'Was the thought that you'd be betraying my father's trust in you the only reason why you didn't come to me last night?'

Muscles ridged along his jaw. His eyelids quivered but he didn't open his eyes.

'Yes,' he admitted slowly between taut lips. 'It was the only reason. Now, go.'

'No.'

His eyes flashed open. She was so close to him now she could see that the little flecks in the dark brown irises appeared red by contrast and as he stared into her eyes it seemed to her that those flecks widened until his eyes glowed fierily.

'You don't know what you're doing,' he whispered, lips still taut. 'When Mason J. Burr hired me he didn't say anything about having to protect you from yourself, from your own wild impulses, nor did he say I would have to fight like hell to keep you at a distance. He didn't tell me that you're a dangerous and fascinating woman, an irresistible temptress. For your own sake, Carlotta, more than mine, will you get to hell out of here?'

Sweat glistened on his shoulders and on the warm brown column of his neck. Giving in to temptation that was also wrecking her last few restraints, Carlotta put a hand on his right shoulder, sliding it over his moist skin. His teeth snapped together as he snarled at her, his lips only a few inches from hers.

'Get out. Go away. Leave me alone.'

She bent her head, the silken wiriness of her hair brushing his face and put her lips to the pulsing hollow at the base of his throat. His skin was salt-tasting. Desire zig-zagged through her, seeming to rip apart all control. Lifting her head a little, she looked up at him through his lashes.

'I can't go now,' she murmured. 'I've fallen in love with you and I want you. You don't really want me to go away and leave you alone now, do you?'

He swore at her, but she could tell he wasn't intending to insult her. He was swearing at himself more than at her.

'Have you any idea what you do to a man when you look at him like that?' he groaned. 'You did it last night on the deck at the Carters' place and I had trouble keeping my hands off you then.'

'You haven't answered my question. Do you really want me to go?' she said, lowering her eyelids, trying not to influence him with a look.

'No, I don't want you to go,' he admitted reluctantly. 'But I think you should.'

'You ought to know by now that I never do what I should do and I always do what I like to do,' she teased him lightly. 'Also, I wouldn't like you to be too bored while you're my bodyguard,' she added.

'For God's sake . . .' he began hoarsely and didn't finish what he was going to say because his lips swooped to hers, swift as an eagle swoops to its prey.

This time he showed no restraint. His tongue thrust into the sweet, moist hollow of her mouth and his fingers closed roughly about her breasts. A series of exquisite sensations corkscrewed through her, right down to the pit of her stomach. Dizzy with desire and heady triumph because she had at last got beneath his guard, she pressed against him eagerly. Her hands twined in his hair to hold his head still so that he couldn't avoid her response to his kiss. Deftly, his hands at her waist, he shifted himself and her until they were lying facing each other on the narrow bunk, their mouths clinging, their breasts touching, their legs entwining.

The yacht plunged on, through and over waves. Water still swished along the smooth hull and gurgled in the forward scuppers. Up and down the bunk tilted, rolling a little from side to side, but lying close to Brad Carlotta heard nothing of the sound of water, felt nothing of the pitch and roll.

Swept by passion as sudden and intense as a tropical squall into a purely sensual word of chaotic nerve-tingling caresses, her mind

drugged with the scent of human hair and
sunkissed skin, her ears deafened by her
own heartbeats, she knew nothing of her
surroundings and cared less. A hunger to
possess and be possessed was consuming her, a
ravenous pagan desire that was swelling and
swelling with every touch of Brad's devastating
fingers, with every nip of his teeth, with every
scorching pressure of his lips against hers.

At first they didn't speak. They were too
breathless. And words weren't needed. Touch
was enough. Skin to skin they shifted against
each other until they were both on fire with
delight and aching to be closer. When Brad did
speak she heard his voice, thick with passion,
faintly through the drumming in her ears.

'Don't be afraid, love. I won't hurt you, but
there's no going back now.'

Wondering vaguely how he knew that, for a
while, she had dreaded that act on the edge of
which they were both teetering, Carlotta
managed to whisper, 'I don't want to back out.
I love you and want you.'

And then suddenly it was over, the part she
had feared most, and she was closer to Brad
than she had ever been. They seemed to be
dancing again, moving in unison, and all the
chaotic sensations were fusing together. Her
head was filled with coloured lights whirling in
the darkness like a strobe light in a discothèque.

The beat of erotic music drummed in her
ears, sensations swam together and swelled in
a huge wave that lifted her up and up.
Everything stopped, the music, her heart, the
revolving coloured lights. Weightless, thought-
less, she floated through space as gentle as a

feather before drifting down to the swish of
water against the hull close beside her, the
slight roll and shudder of the yacht and the
weight of Brad's head on her shoulder, the feel
and taste of his hair in her mouth, the slackness
of his body lying half on and half off her.

Then it came, the feeling of sweet secret
satisfaction because she had got what she had
wanted.

A sudden sharp rap of knuckles on the door
of the cabin made Brad stiffen and roll away
from her. Standing up he snatched up clothing
from the floor, tossed her shirt and shorts on
to her without looking at her and turned away
to pull on his own shorts.

'Who it is?' he yelled and moved to the
door, putting a hand on the knob to hold it
shut if anyone should try to open it.

'Me, man,' Willy's deep voice with its lilting
Caribbean accent answered. 'We're just pulling
into Morrisburg Bay. Skip says to get the line
ready for docking. Hey, man, be looking lively.'

'OK, I'll be with you in a couple of seconds.'

Still half stunned by the completeness of her
capitulation to his love-making, Carlotta lay on
the bunk, her shirt and shorts lying across her
breasts and legs. Through her down-drooping
lashes she watched Brad pull on his T-shirt,
secretly admiring the play of muscle beneath
his skin. For a few moments of passion he had
been hers, entirely hers. She hugged the
knowledge to herself. No matter what happened
now, no matter what cruel jibes he made, she
would remember his loving tenderness during
those few moments for ever.

He thrust his feet into his sneakers and bent

to lace them up. On his way to the door he paused and turned to slant an enquiring glance at her.

'Are you all right?' he asked, and his obviously sincere concern for her well-being touched her heart.

'I'm fine,' she replied smiling at him. 'And you?'

'What do you think?' He parried her question with one of his own as if he didn't want to admit how good he felt.

He turned to the door and grasped hold of the knob then looked back at her again.

'But don't ever try it on with me, again,' he cautioned coldly. 'That clear?'

'Oh, why not?' In the face of his harshness all the lovely warm feeling of fulfilment was fading rapidly.

'Because you and I can't . . .' he started and broke off with a muttered curse, turning his head away from her. 'Oh, hell, because oil and water don't ever mix, I guess,' he added roughly, pushed open the door and stepped into the passage. The door closed with a slam.

Thoroughly confused, Carlotta swung off the bunk and staggered as the yacht changed course sharply, swinging to starboard again. Through the porthole she could see the surface of the sea, red as blood reflecting the sunset. The yacht rolled and she saw a dark headland at the end of which a light was flashing.

While she and Brad had been drowned in passion the sun had dropped below the horizon and the yacht had reached Morunda. Her father had got his way as he usually did. The *Montezuma* would be in its berth at Brock's marina just after six, a few minutes only after the sun had set.

She pulled on her shorts and shirt, thinking of Brad and the final riddle he had flung at her. Oil and water don't mix. Well, she knew that. But who was the oil and who the water? Herself and him, no doubt. And why shouldn't they mix? Hadn't they just proved to each other that they could be fused together in the excitement and pleasure of making love?

But perhaps it hadn't been as pleasurable for him as it had been for her, she thought disconsolately as she left his cabin. After all, she was only a beginner. She wasn't as experienced as he was, and didn't know yet what would give him most pleasure. She could learn, though. She was eager to learn from him, but only from him, and how could she learn from him or about him if they didn't do it again?

Don't try it on with me again. Nasty, sneering words designed to make her hate him.

Why? Oh, forget the bit about oil and water. Forget, too, his excuse about not wanting to betray her father's trust in him. There had to be another reason for his resistance. He didn't love her. Well, she could accept that. She knew men weren't like women. She knew a man didn't have to be in love to make love. She loved him enough to overcome that.

He was probably in love with someone else, a woman in London or even Nassau. A woman to whom he wasn't married, it was true, but with whom he had established a permanent relationship and with whom he was emotionally involved.

As she opened the door of her own cabin and stepped inside it seemed as if her spirits sank to an all-time low. From the dizzy heights of ecstasy to the dark depths of despair in less than fifteen minutes. She sank down on her bunk and stared before her, seeing nothing of the cabin, seeing only the future, her own future, hours, days, months and years of loving Brad while he loved another woman.

CHAPTER NINE

THE bumping of the yacht against the dock, the squeaking sound of fenders as they took the load and the subsequent stopping of the engines all penetrated Carlotta's consciousness and roused her from the cold lethargy into which she had sunk. With a sigh she stood up and went through to the bathroom. She undressed and stepped into the shower stall. She stood under the sluicing hot water for a long time, finding a certain confort in its heat. When she had done she wrapped a towel around herself and returned to the main cabin, found her hair-dryer and plugged it in, thankful that along with all its other luxuries the yacht had two hundred and twenty volt electricity for the running of cookers, refrigerators, water heaters—and her simple hair-dryer.

When her hair was dry she dressed again, this time in narrow white trousers and a loose, navy blue top splattered with white, crimson and blue flowers. Around her hair she wound a long silk scarf, also crimson-coloured, wearing it low on her forehead, and she was just making up her face when someone knocked on the door. Her heart leapt and her cheeks flamed. Could it be Brad, returning from having helped tie the yacht to the dock and stopping on his way to his cabin to explain his riddle and about oil and water?

Knuckles rapped again. A voice called to her. Jilly's voice. Her heart slowed, the colour faded from her cheeks.

'Come in,' she called out and continued to apply lipstick as she held a mirror before her and watched her lips take on the colour of poppies.

'Mr Burr is on board now, miss,' Jilly announced from the open doorway. 'He's in the saloon and would like you to join him and his guests for drinks.'

'Guests?' Carlotta looked up sharply. 'He has guests?'

'Yes. Mr and Mrs Chalmers and Mr and Mrs Digby. Shall I tell Mr Burr you're on your way, miss?'

'Yes—er, yes, please. Tell him . . .' She broke off as a sudden swift thought shot into her mind. 'No, would you mind asking my father, Jilly, if he would come down here? Say there's something I must tell him that's very important and that I can't discuss in front of his guests. Try and make it sound really urgent, Jilly. Because it is.'

'All right, miss. I'll do my best, miss.'

'Thanks.' Carlotta smiled her best and most charming smile. 'You're a dear, Jilly, and you needn't worry. I won't be complaining to him about you, or Skip or about Brad. But I must speak to him in private.'

'Yes, miss.' The anxious lines around Jilly's eyes changed into crinkles of good humour as she smiled back. 'And thank you, miss. Skip and I appreciate what you've just said, miss, and I'd just like to add it's been a pleasure having you on board these past few weeks.'

Jilly went out and closed the door. Flinging

aside the make-up mirror and tube of lipstick,
Carlotta sprang to her feet and began to pace
about the small cabin nervously. What she had
hoped to avoid had happened. Her father had
met Phillida before she had been able to explain
to him about Brad pretending to be Kurt, and
she knew Phillida well enough to realise that the
woman would have no hesitation in telling Mason
Burr she had at last met his son-in-law.

What had been her father's reaction to
Phillida's announcement? She was surprised he
hadn't come storming down to her already to
demand what the hell was going on. But perhaps
that was why he had sent Jilly to ask her to go
up to the saloon. Perhaps he had intended to
confront her about the reappearance of Kurt in
front of Phillida, Gordon and the Digbys, to
surprise and embarrass her into stuttering out
the truth in from of them.

She stopped pacing to linger by the porthole.
The lights from the marina building twinkled in
the dark blue tropical night. She could hear the
familiar beat of of Columbia Rock. There would
be no band at the marina tonight, but the
bartenders would be playing their favourite
numbers on the cassette player. The sound of
the music brought back memories of New Year's
Eve, of herself and Brad sitting on the patio at
separate tables, occasionally glancing at each
other.

Pressing her fists against her temples, she
swung around and began pacing again. Oh, God,
why had she asked him to dance with her? Why
had she given in to that crazy impulse to ask
him to pretend to be her husband? And above
all, why had he gone along with the idea? Had

he been moon-mad too? Had some strange erotic impulse stirred in him? Lonely like her, had he jumped at the chance to dance with someone, to be with someone to celebrate the New Year?

She had only herself to blame for the tangle she was in. She mustn't blame him at all. She had made all the initial moves, even this afternoon. *Don't try it on with me again.* Oh! she gasped painfully as if she had been punched, and sat down on the bunk. Why did he hurt her so? Why was he always rejecting her?

Fingers tapped a tattoo on her door, the knob turned, the door opened and her father looked in. Slim and straight in a well-tailored white tuxedo, his shirt crisply ruffled, his bow tie perfectly arranged and his brushed-back, silvery hair shining under the electric light, he stepped over the sill and closed the door. Leaning against it he looked at her with shrewd grey eyes.

'I believe you have something very important to tell me in private,' he said and his Texan drawl was soft and affectionate.

'Oh, Dad. It's good to see you.' Across the room Carlotta flung herself, her arms going out to him. He caught her against him and kissed her cheek. Tears spurted from her eyes and she hid her face in his shoulder.

'Now, now, sugar. What's all this?' he asked, pushing her gently from him so he could see her face. 'Tears. From you? I thought you despised women who weep.'

'Not any more. I've found out there are times when you have to weep,' she said, sniffing and flicking away the tears from her cheeks with a finger. 'And this is one of them. I . . . thought after that row we had in Vienna you and I would never be friends again, that you would never forgive me for going against your wishes and marrying Kurt.'

'Ah, yes. Kurt,' he murmured. 'He's here, so Phillida tells me. Arrived New Year's Eve.' His grey glance, bright and observant, swept round the cabin. 'I don't see him in here or any signs of his occupancy.' His glance came back to her, his grey eyes hard, brilliant as diamonds. 'Am I to assume he survived the hunting accident and didn't break his neck after all? And are you and he reconciled?'

'Oh, please, Dad, don't go all upstage and haughty on me,' she pleaded. 'Sit down and I'll explain.' He sat down on the settee berth and she sat again on the bunk. 'I hoped to see you before Phillida did, to explain. Kurt was killed, as I told you in my letter. It was an awful shock to me, the news, but I'm over it now and I realise his death solved a lot of problems for me.'

'Then if he's dead, how come Phillida met him on New Year's Eve?' Mason interrupted her.

'I . . . I asked Brad to pretend to be my husband,' she said quickly. 'It . . . it was all I could think of to keep Bernard off my back.'

'Now let's get this straight.' Mason Burr held up a hand and tapped the index finger with the index finger of the other hand. 'First, Brad. I guess you mean Tristan Bradley, the guy I hired to be your bodyguard? Second, Bernard. Would that be Bernard Digby?'

'Right. Dad, Bernie was most . . . well, most obnoxious, pestering me all the time, and to put him off I told him Kurt would be joining me on the yacht on New Year's Eve. So when Bernie turned up here at the marina on New Year's Eve, I asked Brad to dance with me and to pretend to be Kurt if Bernie made himself objectionable.'

'And I guess Bernie made himself objectionable,' drawled Mason. 'So Brad became Kurt.'

'And then Phillida came up to us and we . . . I had to go on with the pretence because Bernie was still there.'

'I see. You mischievous little devil!' he murmured and began to laugh.

'There's more, Dad,' she warned and his face sobered.

'More. OK, tell me the worst,' he said with a sigh of resignation and she told him why Brad had ordered the skipper to leave Morunda to save her the embarrassment of having to explain to Bernard and Phillida that they had been tricked on New Year's Eve, and how they had decided to continue with the pretence when they had gone to the Carters' party.

'Although Tizzy really brought that on herself,' Carlotta complained. 'When she saw Brad she just assumed he was Kurt, fell over herself trying to impress him. It was quite sickening.'

'You like him?' Mason Burr asked abruptly and, realising that she had said more than she had intended, had perhaps given herself away to this shrewd man who was her father, she gave him a quick glance. He was looking at her narrowly.

'Like whom?' she asked, pretending to be surprised.

'Brad. Tristan Bradley.'

'He's . . . he's done his job very professionally,'

she said coolly, but was unable to control the rush of blood to her cheeks. Nor could she look him in the eyes.

'Hmm. Sounds to me as if he's been a tab too professional, pretending to be your husband,' drawled Mason menacingly.

'Oh, you're not to blame him for it!' Carlotta rose to the bait too quickly, giving herself away again, although she didn't realise it. 'It was all my fault. I'm to blame for the mess I'm in now. Dad, what am I going to do about Phillida? When she mentioned that Kurt was with me, what did you say? Did you tell her he was dead?'

'I said nothing,' he replied. 'I have to admit I was a bit shaken but I hope I'm a good enough actor not to have shown it. I let her ramble on and held my peace, thinking I'd find out just exactly what was going on from you first.' He rose to his feet. 'They've gone, Phillida and Gordon and the Digbys, but I said we'd join them for dinner at Jonathan's.' Jonathan's was an all-American restaurant situated on the hill behind the marina. 'You ready to go now?'

'But what am I going to say to Phillida about Brad not being Kurt?'

'Brad doesn't have to come to dinner too,' he said.

'But have you forgotten? He's my bodyguard. He goes everywhere I go.'

'He doesn't have to go where you go tonight,' he drawled, turning to the door. His hand on the knob he turned to her. 'Don't worry about it, honey. All you have to say is that Kurt has gone back to Europe. You can even dress it up a bit and say you and he have had a tiff and you

hope you'll never see him again. Then later in
the year, much later we can let it out to friends
and family that he's dead. It's just a case of
postponing his death.'

'But . . . but supposing Philllida or Bernie sees
Brad, here at the marina? Bernie often comes
down to the bar here and we can't ask Brad to
stay aboard ship all the time,' she exclaimed.

'Leave it to me,' he said firmly. 'I'll have a
word with Brad right now, tell him he doesn't
have to come with us tonight because I'll be
with you. You just remember what you're going
to say to Phillida and the others when they ask
where Kurt is. It will work out OK, honey. I
promise you. Now where will I find Brad?'

'Probably in his cabin. Number four in the
fo'c'sle,' she said dully. Then, on a sudden
thought she sprang to her feet. 'But you won't
sack him, will you, Dad? Please.'

'Just leave it to me, sugar,' he said soothingly.
'Everything will be all right. I'll join you in a
few minutes in the saloon before going ashore.'

He was much longer than a few minutes, and
she had been waiting in the saloon nearly half
an hour, pacing up and down nervously,
wondering what was being said below decks,
fearful that her father might do the very thing
she had tried to avoid and would sack Brad.
Several times she thought of going down to
Brad's cabin to interfere, but every time she
controlled the impulse. Hard experience had
taught her to be careful where her father was
concerned. If she showed too much interest in
Brad he would guess she had fallen in love with
her bodyguard and he would do everything in
his power to stop the affair.

When Mason eventually appeared she tried to appear unconcerned, although she observed his face closely for any signs of anger. But he was too good a poker player to betray any signs of emotion, and in the end she had to ask, as they left the yacht and walked along the dock, if everything was all right.

'Sure it's all right. We had a good laugh over your little charade. I explained to him what we were going to do about it tonight and he agreed that it was a good idea. So that's that.'

'But . . . supposing Phillida and Bernie see Brad while the yacht is still here?'

'They won't. You see, sugar, that's why I flew down today. We're leaving Morunda in the morning and going over to the Virgin Islands. Cora and Granny Liz are flying to St Thomas today and will join us there. Then we'll go over to the island of Culobra to visit the Erlandsons and from there cruise the south coast of Puerto Rico before making for the Bahamas. I'd like Atkins to take the yacht back to Texas for the spring. It needs some attention. You'll come on the cruise with us, of course.'

'I suppose so,' she murmured.

Jonathan's turned out to be a good choice of place in which to meet Phillida, Gordon and the Digbys, Carlotta thought later, when she sat at a table in a long room with a cathedral ceiling that looked out from the hillside over the light-twinkling harbour to the dark shapes of hills on the other shore. It was full of American tourists, and the noise of their loud voices filled the room. To make oneself heard by one's neighbour one had to shout.

Phillida seemed to lose interest in the subject

of Kurt when Carlotta told her that he had
returned to Europe, and it wasn't necessary to
say anything about having quarrelled with him.
Since there were some acquaintances from New
York at the table also, Phillida was much more
interested in them. Bernard, Carlotta learned
from his parents, had returned to the States.
Soon it seemed to her that she had worried
about nothing, and when she lay on her bunk
later that night, sleepless, the panic she had
experienced at seeing Bernard on New Year's
Eve, which had driven her into asking Brad to
dance with her and to masquerade as her
husband, seemed now to have been part of a
dream.

But had she asked Brad to dance with her
only because she had seen a way to avoid
Bernard? With a groan she faced up to the
reality of her feelings about Brad. Why not
admit that she had been attracted to him from
the first time she had seem him when she had
come aboard the yacht at the beginning of
December? For a month she had watched him
covertly, had felt a certain thrill of excitement
whenever she had noticed him in a street or
disco, and had wondered then if he had been
following her because he had been attracted to
her too.

Now she knew he had been following her for
an entirely different reason. He had followed
her to protect her. There was something very
romantic about having a bodyguard like him,
she thought dreamily, and wished he would be
around to protect her for ever from men like
Bernard, or even Kurt. She wished Brad could

be her *real* husband. But that was something that seemed beyond her reach now.

She slept little as she tussled with this new problem, slipping into slumber only towards dawn. She woke later to the sound of the yacht's engines. Hurrying, she showered and dressed and went up to the saloon. The yacht was well out to sea and the hills of Morunda were sinking fast below the line of the eastern horizon. Ahead the sea stretched glittering with sunlight, green, turquoise and purple, moving perpetually under the arching cloudless blue sky.

'Mr Burr and Skip have already had breakfast,' Jilly announced as she came into the saloon. 'I'm sorry I didn't have time to wake you earlier with some juice, miss. I had to help with the dock lines.'

'Why was that? I thought Brad always helped Willy with the lines,' said Carlotta.

'Brad isn't with us any more. He left yesterday evening for Antigua, soon after you'd gone ashore,' replied Jilly.

Shock made Carlotta sit down suddenly on one of the chairs. She watched Jilly pour coffee for her.

'Do you know why he left?' she asked when she could speak.

'He just said the time had come for him to leave.'

'He wasn't sacked, was he, Jilly?' Carlotta asked hoarsely.

'Not as far as I know. He and your dad parted on good terms, I believe. I gather you didn't complain to Mr Burr about Brad's behaviour.'

'No, I didn't.' She discovered she was feeling cold. The coffee she had gulped down was tasteless and no help at all. Jilly, do you know where he's gone?' she whispered.

Jilly glanced at her, a slight frown pleating her brow.

'Are you all right, miss? You're looking a bit pale. Don't feel sick, do you? They say there's been a lot of food poisoning on the island. Some of those restaurants aren't too hygienic and the kitchen staff aren't as particular as they could be about the preparation of food and so much of the meat is frozen and then not cooked thoroughly.'

'No. I'm not sick, Jilly. But I don't think I'll have anything to eat. I suppose my father is in the wheelhouse?'

'That's right, miss. He says we're going to pick up Mrs Burr and your grandmother in St Thomas. I'm really looking forward to meeting the old lady again.'

'So am I,' said Carlotta, brightening up a little and sliding off the berth. 'I'll go and join Dad,' she murmured.

Her heart felt like a lump of lead in her chest as she mounted the steps to the wheelhouse. Or was it just the cold coffee lying unswallowed somewhere in her gullet, she wondered with a wry grin at herself? She slid open the door to the wheelhouse and entered its air-conditioned coolness. Her father was alone, looking through his binoculars at a freighter that was coming towards the yacht, and the automatic pilot was steering. From the VHF came the sound of a voice calling the harbour master at Morrisburg from another yacht.

'Did you fire Brad last night?' Carlotta attacked right away.

Mason lowered the binoculars and turned to smile at her. He leaned towards her and kissed her on one cheeks.

'Morning, sugar. So you've finally decided to shake a leg,' he drawled. 'I thought you'd be up at sunrise and ready to go.'

'I didn't sleep too well,' she excused herself. 'But don't dodge the issue, Dad. Did you or didn't you give Brad the sack last night?'

'No, I didn't. I promised you I wouldn't. When I went to see him he was packing up to leave. That was the arrangement he and I had, that he would leave us as soon as I arrived.' He raised the glasses to his eyes and looked at the freighter. 'Guess we're on a collision course with this guy and I'd best go to starboard of him. He has the right of way.'

He went to the instrument panel and turned a knob. Slowly the bow of the yacht swung to the right.

'Why wasn't I told of this arrangement you and Brad had?' demanded Carlotta shakily. 'Why didn't you tell me last evening?'

He didn't reply but raised the binoculars to his eyes again to watch the freighter going by on the port side of the yacht.

'Answer my question, please,' she insisted. 'And stop treating me as if I were a child. I'm all grown up now and can be told unpleasant truths. It's all right. I won't rush off in a huff and do anything you wouldn't like. I learned my lesson when I married Kurt against your advice. Please, Dad, why didn't you tell me you had that arrangement with Brad?'

He lowered the glasses again, turned the knob

on the instrument panel and the yacht's bow swung back on to the original course.

'I guess I thought he'd told you the other day after he'd talked to me and asked my permission to tell you why he'd been hired,' he replied smoothly. He gave her a sidelong glance. 'Were you mad when you found out he'd been hired as a bodyguard?'

'A little, but when he explained why I understood. I was really only mad at you for not telling me about those threats and taking me into your confidence, consulting me before hiring anyone to protect me.'

'I was anxious about you, honey. I had to do something quickly. I asked Skip to get in touch with Brad, to find out if he was still in Nassau and to ask him if he knew of anyone in the Caribbean area who could do the job of protecting you. Seems that Skip just caught Brad as he was getting ready to leave Nassau and fly to England. He'd finished working for the Bahamian police and was going home for Christmas. He didn't know of anyone suitable he could recommend to be your bodyguard but offered to come to Morunda, work on the yacht and keep an eye on you until I was able to get away or found someone who could take on the job of being your bodyguard permanently. I jumped at his offer. I'm sorry if you were miffed at not being consulted, but sometimes it's necessary to take action without consulting everyone involved. I did it for your safety. Does that answer your question?'

'I guess so,' she sighed. 'Have you found someone to be my permanent bodyguard?'

'No. And I'm not looking any more. The guy

who wrote the threatening letters has been found. He's some crazy nut who's got a grudge against the company because he was fired for not doing his work properly. He decided to take his revenge through me and you, although neither or us had anything to do with the hiring and firing of him. I guess you don't need a bodyguard . . .' he broke off then added drily, 'until the next time.'

'I'm glad I don't need a bodyguard any more and I hope there won't be a next time,' she said with vehement sincerity. 'But I'm sorry Brad had to leave so suddenly. He . . . he said he would try to let me know if . . . if there was to be a change, if he thought up some way of getting out of the embarrassment of us having to tell Phillida we had deceived her.'

'He said I was to say goodbye to you,' Mason replied, studying a sailing yacht they were passing. There wasn't much wind and the black-hulled, tan-sailed ketch was rolling idly on the sun-shimmered water. The helmsman raised his hand to wave to them. They waved back. 'I invited Brad to stay on as a guest to come to the Virgins and Puerto Rico, but he declined. He said he had to get back to England immediately.' Mason fiddled with the binoculars, adjusting the focus of the lens. He added casually, 'He's a nice guy, a helluva nice guy.'

'Yes, he is,' Carlotta mumbled and stared unseeingly out of the wide, grey-tinted glass at the distant horizon. She had thought she had plumbed the depths of despair last evening. But this feeling was worse. This was like being alive and dead at the same time.

A movement on the foredeck below the

wheelhouse drew her attention. Willy was
sauntering along the deck towards the bow. He
stopped to lean on the bulwark and looked over
at the sparkling bow-wave. But no tall man with
sun-bleached, dark brown hair followed him to
lean beside him. Brad had left, was even now
almost home, almost back in England, perhaps.
He was miles away. A whole ocean separated
him from her. Carlotta drew a long, shaky breath
and let it out.

'What's wrong, honey?' Mason as always was
quick to notice any emotional disturbance in his
one and only child.

'Nothing much. I just wish . . .' She broke off
and sighed again.'

'Go on. What do you wish?'

'That I wasn't a rich girl. That I was just an
ordinary woman, with a career or some sort of
work to do. I wish I had more freedom.' She
turned to him. 'I'm glad I don't have to have a
bodyguard any more. I'm glad you're here, too.
It's such a long time since we were together.
There's so much I want to talk to you about.'

'And I'm glad too, that you feel you want to
talk to me,' he said, rather humbly for Mason J.
Burr II, she thought. 'I guess I was a bit rough
with you that day in Vienna.'

'Rough but right,' she admitted. 'I know now
you were doing your best to prevent me from
making a mistake. But you know, Dad, Granny
Liz has always said about you that you only ever
learned from making your own mistakes. Guess
I must be like you.'

'Could be you are,' he agreed. 'Could be too,
as my mother has pointed out to me more than
once, I'm too possessive of you, over-protective

too. But you see, Carlo, you're all I have left of my love affair and marriage with your mother. And then with being my heiress and all, it's only natural that I should want to try and stop you from falling into the traps set by creeps like Kurt Malden.'

'I understand that, and I guess I won't be any different when I'm a parent . . . if I ever am. But I can't help wishing I weren't your heiress. Life would be much simpler for me if I weren't. It would be easier to judge then if . . . if a man wanted to marry me because he really loved me. Do you understand what I'm getting at, Dad?'

'Only too well.' He laughed a little self-mockingly. 'Remember I was your grandfather's only son and heir. Come to think of it, I had this same discussion with him, when I was about twenty-one or two.'

'What did he do?'

'Sent me to work for the company as a rigger at an oil exploration site in the Arctic. Stopped paying me an allowance so that I had to learn to live on any income I earned. Made it known that I wouldn't be inheriting all he owned when he died.' He slanted her a glance. 'Is that what you want me to do? Cut your allowance, tell everyone you're not going to inherit billions of dollars?'

'You did threaten to do that when you found out I'd married Kurt,' she pointed out.

'It was a threat only and it was directed at him. And it worked, didn't it? Showed him up in his true colours?'

'Well, I've no wish to be an oil-rigger,' she said with a little laugh. Talking with him about her own situation like this was easing the cold leaden feeling, the feeling that something in her had died. 'I'm not that liberated. But I would like to see if I could do a job, earn an income and manage on it. I'm tired of being a little rich girl with nothing to do. The problem is I'm not much good at anything. I only know how to look after horses and ride them. I guess I'm pretty good at mucking out and riding.' She paused as a sudden idea flashed into her mind but decided not to tell him about it. Not yet. Not until she had written a letter and received an answer to it. Not until she was sure she had a job at a certain riding stables she knew of in England.

'Mucking out horses. Ha!' Mason's short laugh was derisive. 'Jobs don't come much dirtier than that. You could start your own riding school in Texas. I could finance you!'

'No. No. That's what I *don't* want! I have to go away, work somewhere on my own. You're not to come running with help, financial or otherwise. I'd like you to carry out your threat to stop my allownace—I haven't spent all you've given me, I've saved some and that will get me going. And I'd be very much obliged if you'd put it about that I'm not going to inherit all your millions. I don't want all of them anyway. There would be too much for just me.'

'My inheritance and yours, the ranch, the shares in the oil company aren't just for you, honey,' he argued softly. 'It's for your kids and their kids . . .'

'I won't be having any kids the way I'm going on,' she retorted suddenly losing patience. 'The way things are right now I'll never find the right guy to marry. Nice guys don't go hunting for rich girls.'

He swung to face her, grey eyes narrowing assessingly.

'You liked him a lot, didn't you?' he drawled. 'Too much.'

'What . . . what . . . who are you talking about?' she whispered blustering a little, realising at last that she had given herself away.

'You know what and who, honey,' he said drily. 'But you'll get over it. I wouldn't mind betting that by the end of next week you'll be over it. You always do get over these infatuations of yours in a few days.'

Her impulse was to flare up at him, to retort angrily, but just in time she remembered that was what she had done when he had warned her about Kurt. Now he had guessed how she felt about Brad and he was warning her again, not against Brad but against her own waywardness and changeability.

'Perhaps you're right,' she heard herself saying coolly. 'But that doesn't alter how I feel about being independent. Please, Dad, consider what I've said seriously. I don't want to have to go and find my way in the world without your blessing. I want us to stay friends. But I will go, I promise you that.'

'OK, I'm hearing you,' he replied with a touch of irritability. 'But you're not going yet. Wait until the end of this cruise we're going to take with Cora and Granny Liz. Talk over what it is you want to do with Granny. She has a lot of wisdom and her advice is worth taking.'

'Oh, I will, I will talk it over with her,' she said fervently. She was looking forward to seeing her grandmother, who had stepped in and taken the place of her mother when Juanita had died so tragically. Granny Liz was bound to be on her side in any arguments with Mason.

She glanced down at the foredeck again. Willy was still there leaning on the rail and now she imagined someone was beside him, as tall, wide-shouldered man. Then the tall man turned. Sunlight glinted on the streaks in his dark hair. He looked up at the wheelhouse and it seemed to her he looked right at her and gave her the thumbs-up sign.

Her father spoke to her. The figure faded. Only Willy was there. She turned with a smile to answer Mason's question. She was feeling better. An ocean might separate her physically from Brad but something of him had remained with her, in the depths of her heart.

CHAPTER TEN

ON the first day of March, at the end of
the cruise with her father, stepmother and
grandmother, Carlotta left the yacht at Nassau
and flew to England. She travelled light, taking
with her the minimum of clothing. Her life as
the spoiled heiress of Mason J. Burr was over.
From that day on she would be an independent
woman fending for herself and living on the
small income she would earn as a riding instructor
and stablehand at the stables in Berkshire owned
by her grandmother's niece, Grace Heward.

Because she was just starting work at the
stables, Grace let her live with her and her
family in the old farmhouse where once Granny
Liz had lived and grown up with her sister,
Grace's mother, but by the end of May Carlotta
had found separate accommodation and was
sharing a small cottage in the nearby village with
one of the other riding instructors, Sarah Goodall.

Although she had found going to work
restrictive and routine at first, she had found
many compensations working with the animals
she loved and with companions with whom she
had much in common. There had been pleasure
too in watching spring work its magic on the
English countryside, as drifts of daffodils had
yellowed the grass in the orchard at Greenacres,

to be followed in May by the pale petals of
fallen apple blossom. Lambs had been born to
the few sheep Grace kept, and two new foals
had been delivered in the stables. A robin had
built its nest in the tangled garden of the cottage,
and now swallows were flitting to and from the
eaves.

Most of all Carlotta had enjoyed the privacy.
No one at the stables or in the village knew she
was the daughter of a billionaire oil tycoon. She
was just a distant relative of Grace's from the
States, a little different, it was true, with her
drawling accent, her outspoken comments and
her impulsive demonstrations of affection, but
after the first few days she had been accepted
and more or less ignored. Life was suddenly
simple, there in the greenness of Berkshire. Her
only social activity was a visit to the village pub
on a Friday night with Grace and her husband
Tom.

Slowly but surely the disasters of the previous
months slipped from her mind. Kurt was
forgotten. Bernard Digby was forgotten. Even
Tizzy and Ethan had become vague. She was
still hoping to forget Brad, but was reluctant to
blot from her mind their crazy masquerade on
New Year's Eve. Often when she was restless
she would relive those moments when she had
danced with him, and the way he had kissed her
then and later on the shore at the Bay of Doves.
Only when her memory began to remind her of
the last time they had been together in his cabin
did she open her eyes and try to think of
something else. She didn't want to remember
the remarks he had made when he had left her.

One afternoon in June, after the last of the

junior classes she had been instructing had
finished, she sat in the tack-room, among the
saddles and bridles, examining a bridle that had
broken during the class. The door was pushed
open and a man's voice said, 'I've come to pick
up Joanna Martin. Do you know where she is?'

Carlotta gripped the bridle tightly, holding on
to it as the only real thing to grasp. Was she
going out of her mind? The voice sounded
exactly like Brad's: cool, crisp. She looked up
slowly at the doorway. She wasn't out of her
mind. He was there, looking bigger somehow in
a brown leather jacket, open-necked shirt and
jeans. She stared at him feeling her heart begin
to race and the blood to steal into her cheeks.
He stared back.

'Carlotta?' he queried.

'Yes. It's me . . . I'm Carlotta,' she stammered
and stood up. 'Joanna is in the stable, feeding
sugar to her pony, I guess.'

His dark glance flashed over her in the way
she remembered taking in her tightly bound
hair, her sagging old sweatshirt and her stained
jodhpurs and boots, before returning to her face.
Kicking the door shut behind him, he stepped
over to the table at which she was sitting.

'I didn't recognise you at first,' he said. 'You
look a lot different from when I last saw you.'
Again his glance frisked her. 'What are you
doing here?' he asked.

'Isn't it obvious? I work here as a riding
instructor.'

She sat down again because she felt suddenly
weak. The room was vibrating with tension. She
had a longing to fling her arms around him to
hug him, she was so excited by seeing him again,

but the memory of one of his last remarks was
still branded on her mind. *Don't try it on with
me again.*

'It's unbelievable,' he murmured, and shook
his head from side to side so that the long lock
of hair slid over his forehead. The sun-bleached
strands weren't as noticeable and he wasn't
tanned any more. He looked as if he spent a lot
of his time working indoors.

'What is? That I'm working? Or that I'm
working here at these stables? I suppose you
always have thought I'm incapable of working
for my living and that I'm just a playgirl,' she
challenged him.

'I suppose I have,' he replied, his eyes glinting.
'You certainly never did anything when I was
with you to make me think otherwise!'

The longing to hug him and kiss him died a
violent death under the rush of an urge to slap
him for insulting her. She suppressed it with
difficulty and, turning away from him, picked up
the broken bridle.

'You'd best go and find Joanna,' she said
coldly. 'Good afternoon, Mr Bradley.'

He made no reply. She didn't look up but she
heard the latch of the door rattle as he lifted it.
Then the door slammed shut and he was gone.
Alone, she subsided shakily, folding her arms on
the table and putting her head down on them.
The unexpected meeting with Brad had shaken
her more than she would have believed possible.

The latch rattled and she straightened up quickly.
The door opened and Grace came in. Younger
looking than her forty-odd years, she was lean
and flat-chested. Her fair hair was scraped back
from her long thin face into a tight bun at the

back of her neck. She looked severe but her
blue-grey eyes sparkled with humour.

'It's Colley's birthday today so I thought we'd
take her out to dinner at the village pub tonight.
Are you game?' she asked. Colley was one of
the three riding instructors employed at the
stables. 'Oh, dear, what's the matter?' The
sparkle died in Grace's eyes as she glanced at
Carlotta. 'You're as white as a ghost.'

'Perhaps that's because I've just seen one,'
replied Carlotta, her voice unsteady. 'Did you
see him, the man who just walked out of here?
You must have passed him.'

'Yes, I did, as a matter of fact,' said Grace
hitching a leg up on the corner of the table
while she still studied Carlotta's white face. 'He
nearly knocked me over. He seemed pretty angry
about something. I've seen him before. Who is
he? Did he come in here to see you?'

'He's Tristan Bradley and he didn't come to
see me. He's come to pick up Joanna Martin. I
suppose it's all right to let her go with him?'

'I expect he's come instead of her mother, Pat
Martin. It's with her I've seen him occasionally,
in Ascot. Gossip has it that they cohabit. You
know what I mean? I've really no idea how to
describe a relationship between a man and a
woman when it's something like marriage but
you know they aren't married, at least not to
each other.' Grace paused and frowned a little.
'Now I come to think about it, Joanna could be
his child. She does resemble him a little.' She
looked across at Carlotta again. 'But that doesn't
account for you thinking you saw a ghost when
he came in here. Where and when did you meet
him before?'

'In Morunda, when I was living on the yacht at the beginning of January.'

'Really? Well, what a coincidence him walking in and finding you here,' said Grace lightly.

'Yes, wasn't it,' murmured Carlotta, wondering whether it had been a coincidence. Was it possible Brad had known she was here at the stables? Who could have told him? Anyway, why would he go out of his way to come and see her? He had left her in no doubt, as usual, how he felt about her. She hurried after Grace and into the stableyard. A dark blue car was just driving away. From the passenger seat in front, dark-eyed and dark-haired, Joanna Martin waved to her and Grace. They both waved back.

'Grace, he knows about me,' Carlotta whispered as she walked with her cousin towards the farmhouse. Built of local reddish-brown brick, its old-fashioned sash windows outlined in white, it glowed in the sunlight of late afternoon among its attendant elm trees. 'He knows I'm Dad's heiress. I hope he doesn't tell Pat Martin who I am. I wouldn't want it to get around the village. I've been so happy living here, anonymous and ignored.'

'I wouldn't worry about her spreading gossip. She keeps very much to herself,' said Grace serenely. 'Now what time shall Tom and I pick you and Sarah up this evening?

Although Carlotta did her best to push the meeting with Brad to the back of her mind, it would keep forcing itself to the front. She tried hard to be merry at the dinner party and thought she was succeeding until she saw Brad walk into the pub's dining-room accompanied by a slim dark-haired, dark-eyed woman. Watching the

couple covertly as they sat down at one of the
dark oak tables, she nudged Grace.

'Is that Pat Martin?' she whispered. 'Look,
over there. The table by the second window.'

Grace glanced around casually.

'Yes, that's her. And him. She's quite pretty,
isn't she, but older than I had thought. Not
much younger than I am, is my guess.' Grace
turned back to the table and said sharply as
Carlotta struggled to her feet, 'What are you
doing? Where are you going?'

'I'm getting out of here,' muttered Carlotta.
'Sorry, Colley, Grace . . . I've just remembered
something I have to do. See you tomorrow. See
you later, Sarah.'

'Carlotta, you can't . . .' began Grace severely,
but Carlotta paid no heed. The sight of Brad
with another woman was proving too much for
her just as the sight of him sitting with Tizzy had
been one moonlit tropical night nearly six months
ago. Jealousy was raging through her. She
couldn't sit passively and see him smile at Pat
Martin across candlight. It was more than she
could bear.

Once she had left the pub she turned along
the lane to the cottage she shared with Sarah,
forgetting she was wearing high heels, the first
time for months. Finding she couldn't walk fast
enough she took the shoes off and walked in her
stockinged feet even though every tiny loose
stone pricked her soles. As she walked she
looked up at the starlit sky, at the moon, only in
its first quarter and smaller than it was in the
tropics. It was a lovely night, quiet, peaceful, an
English midsummer's night when the fairies were

supposed to come out and play havoc with the
love lives of poor humans.

Well, they were certainly out tonight, Carlotta
thought wryly as she let herself into the cottage.
They had waved their wands and Brad had
appeared, and now all the peace of mind she
had worked so hard these past few months to
achieve was gone. He had stepped into the tack-
room that afternoon and the attraction she felt
for him had been triggered off again. Of all the
coincidences she could have imagined it was the
last one she had expected when she had come to
live in England. The chances of him coming to
the place where she worked not knowing she
was there were tens of thousands to one. No,
more like a million to one. But if he had known,
had found out in some way that she was working
at Greenacres, why had he come to the stables?
Just to check up on the information he had
received that a young woman called Carlotta
Burr was working there? Was it possible Joanna
Martin—who could be his daughter, according
to Grace—had mentioned her riding instructor's
name to him?

That was it. That had to be it. He had heard
her name at the home of his . . . his paramour,
his mistress—God, what should she call Pat
Martin? In the silence of her bedroom Carlotta
ground her teeth. He had heard her name and
had come to check her out and now he was
probably telling Pat Martin all about her,
laughing about her . . .

But he wouldn't tell Pat about their brief and
tumultuous mating in his cabin aboard the
Montezuma, would he? Oh, no. He wouldn't
tell her of his physical conquest of the young

woman whose bodyguard he had been for a few
short weeks. Men were usually very secretive
about such things. And often forgot them. As
she must forget, as she was going to forget.

She slept badly and was tired and absent-
minded the next day, going through the motions
only of instructing children in how to ride. She
left the stables late, long after Sarah had gone
and walked back to the cottage slowly, in spite
of the rain that had begun to fall.

She was quite a way from the cottage when a
car coming the opposite way stopped beside her.
The window rolled down and Brad looked out at
her as he leaned over from the driver's seat. He
pushed the door open.

'Get in,' he ordered.

'No, thanks. I've only a short way to go.'

'You'll get soaked.'

'I don't care.' She began to walk on. Behind
her she heard the car door slam and expected
to hear it move off, but instead she heard
footsteps coming after her. Defensively she
turned to face him.

'Carlotta, don't be silly,' he began, but his
voice was soft and the little reddish flecks in
his eyes had begun to glow. Grace was right,
Joanna did resemble him a little, especially
around the eyes. The implication of that
resemblance hit her a hard and unexpected
blow.

'But I am silly. And you know that . . .'

'You're bloody stubborn,' he growled at her.
'Come and get in the car. I'd like to talk to
you. I was just driving out to the stables to see
if you were still there.'

'There's nothing to talk about. We have

nothing to say to each other, Mr Tristan
Bradley,' she said haughtily.

'Who told you my first name?' he demanded,
looking disconcerted for a moment.

'My father. Goodbye.' She turned on her
heel and began to walk on, pretending that
one of her riding boots wasn't pinching her
little toe.

Suddenly she was seized from behind. His
hands at her waist he lifted her and threw her
over his shoulder in a fireman's lift.

'Stop it, you bully,' she gasped hitting his
back with both fists. 'Put me down.'

A car coming along the lane drew to a stop
beside them. A man's voice asked if they
needed help.

'No, thanks,' said Brad easily, turning to the
man so that Carlotta was swung dizzily in the
opposite direction. 'My wife has twisted her
ankle and I'm just carrying her to the car.'

'OK.'

The car's window was closed, and the vehicle
moved away slowly.

'Help, help,' yelled Carlotta breathlessly and
almost at once she was lowered to her feet.
They were right beside Brad's car.

'Shut up,' he snarled viciously, still holding
on to her.

'Help, help,' she screeched. 'I'm being
kidnapped.'

A sharp jerk and she was against him, breast
to breast. Hard and domineering his lips came
down on hers, smothering her next shout before
it started.

The shock of his kiss, the unexpectedness of
it also defeated any resistance in her before

she could make it. Her lips parted involuntarily as she sighed with a feeling compounded of delight and sudden amusement at this latest escapade of theirs. She leaned against him frankly, raised her hands to his nape and gave in to the sensuous pleasure of being kissed by him. After a while, when they both were becoming aware that the rain was soaking their hair, and drenching their clothing, Brad lifted his mouth from hers. His dark eyes blazed with fire.

'I had no intention of kissing you when I stopped to give you a lift,' he murmured.

'And I had no intention of being kissed by you,' she whispered. 'We couldn't help it.'

'It happened because you don't know how to behave in an English country lane on a Sunday afternoon,' he said roughly. 'Yelling for help like that.'

'Well, what about you? Heaving me over your shoulder as if I was . . . a sack of potatoes,' she seethed. 'Kidnapping me.'

He laughed softly and, raising a hand, wiped the rain from one of her cheeks with a forefinger. At that remembered heart-touching caress her knees shook. She wanted to shout at him not to do it again, but all she could do was stare at him as if mesmerised by the expression of tenderness that had softened the hard lines of his face.

'I've missed you, Carlotta, and I've been anxious about you,' he murmured.

'Anxious about me? Why?' she exclaimed.

Immediately his face pokered up. It was as if, for a moment, he had allowed her a glimpse of someone she didn't know and had never

met and then had swiftly drawn down the
blinds. His face took on its usual expression,
eyes narrow and wary, line of mouth tightly
controlled.

'I can't tell you here, while we're getting
rained on. Isn't there somewhere we could go
to talk for a while? Somewhere out of the
rain?' he asked.

'You can come to the cottage. I share it with
Sarah. It's very small, though. And you'll have
to duck your head as you go through the
doorway.'

'It couldn't be any smaller than my cabin on
the *Montezuma*,' he said drily and, turning
away, he opened the nearest door of the car.
'Will you condescend now to get in?' he
drawled mockingly.

The drive to the cottage took no more than
four minutes. After parking the car on the
grass verge of the road, Brad followed her
along the flagged pathway between the tangled
flower beds to the plain front door under the
little peaked roof of the porch. He stood close
beside her as she unlocked the door. Inside
she lingered long enough in the narrow, dark-
panelled hallway to open the door to Sarah's
room to check whether or not her friend was
in. The room was empty so she closed the door
and went over to the door opposite.

As she entered her own room she whispered
to Brad, 'Don't forget to duck.'

Since it was such a damp evening she switched
on the electric fire and the simulated flames
began to flicker. A table lamp with a pink
shade dispersed gathering shadows and folk-
weave curtains pulled across the window blotted

out the greyness outside. Low-ceilinged, with heavy beams, the room was furnished with a wide settee, an armchair and a small, round dining table set under the window. In an alcove behind a curtain on one side of the fireplace were a sink and an electric cooker. On the other side of the fireplace was the door to the bedroom.

'Shall I shut the door?' Brad asked.

'Yes. And take off your jacket. The shoulders are wet. Hang it over one of those chairs,' Carlotta, determined to be practical, gestured towards the two Windsor chairs at the table. 'I'll get you a towel to dry your hair.'

Fifteen minutes later, her own hair drying and beginning to glint with golden sparks she sat curled up in the armchair. Brad sat down on the settee, leaned back, thrust his hands in his pockets and stretched his long legs before him, crossing his ankles. He looked up at the beams.

'This place must be quite old.' he said non-committally.

'About three hundred years, Grace says.'

'Grace?' His glance came down from the ceiling and focused on her.

'You know, she owns and runs the stables,' she replied coolly and went straight to the point. 'Brad, I have to ask you. Was it just coincidence we met this afternoon. Or did you know I was working at the stables?'

'I knew you . . . or I had heard that a Carlotta Burr was working there,' he said smoothly—too smoothly, she thought.

'So you came yesterday afternoon to check me out.'

'Right.'

'I suppose your . . . I mean, Joanna, mentioned my name.'

'She may have done.' He shrugged.

'She resembles you a little,' she murmured, rubbing at a spot on the knee of her jodhpurs, avoiding his gaze and feeling again the jealousy she had experienced the previous night in the pub's dining-room warping her thoughts. 'Is she your daughter?' As she spoke she flung back her head to look directly at him again.

'My what? Good God, no!' He sat up straight and stared at her. 'Where in hell did you get that idea?'

'Oh, it doesn't matter who suggested it to me, does it? You're very chummy with Joanna's mother, so it was a reasonable conclusion to draw from the child's resemblance to you,' she replied coolly, looking down at the spot on her knee again but watching him closely through the silky screen of her lashes.

'I see. Oh, I see very well,' he drawled, mockery glinting in his eyes. 'You've been listening to gossip. Pat told me there was talk about my regular visits to see her at the weekends and we had a good laugh about it.' He leaned back again but the mockery still danced in his eyes. 'So now I understand why you swept out of the pub last night, soon after we arrived.'

'I hadn't realised you'd seen me—you were so busy smiling at her, helping her to choose from the menu,' she said stiffly. 'I left because I didn't feel too well.'

'You'll always fail a lie detector test,' he jeered. 'You left the pub because you didn't like me paying more attention to Pat than to you. I haven't forgotten how you behaved the night we visited the Carters at Stenson Point. You haven't changed, Carlotta. You still show everything you feel, do everything up front, as they say in your country.' He gave her one of his dark, intent glances. 'And I'm glad,' he added softly.

'Is . . . is Pat Martin your mistress?' she asked.

He uttered his usual crisp oath and gave her a different glance, one that scorched her with scorn.

'Pat is my elder sister,' he replied.

'Oh.' She felt silly and relieved at the same time. 'You visit her a lot.'

'Because she's on her own a lot. Her husband is a master mariner, captains an oil tanker and is away months at a time,' he explained.

'Oh,' she said again, and felt herself colouring as she met the mockery glinting in his eyes.

'Feel better now?' he taunted.

'A little,' she admitted. 'Why . . . why didn't you tell me you would be leaving the *Montezuma* as soon as my father arrived?' she continued, returning to the attack.

'I'm not sure.' He spoke slowly, avoiding her eyes. 'Maybe I felt it was wiser not to.' He shrugged.

'And you broke your promise to let me know as soon as you thought up a way of avoiding telling Phillida about our masquerade, too,' she complained.

'There wasn't time to tell you or to say goodbye to you,' he said stiffly.

'I thought you left in a hurry because you

were glad to get out of an involvement with
me,' she persisted. 'I guessed you'd regretted
what had happened in your cabin from what
you said to me about not trying it on again
with you. You blamed me for what happened.
You couldn't leave fast enough.'

'I left because I had to,' he interrupted her
roughly. 'When we returned to Morunda there
was a cable waiting for me at the marina. It
was from my sister with the news that my
father had died suddenly and asking me to fly
home at once. That was why I left without
saying goodbye to you. Mason made his plane
and pilot available to me to fly me to Antigua
that evening so I could catch a flight to Britain
the next day.'

'Oh.' She felt even more deflated. 'He didn't
tell me,' was all she could say. 'I'm sorry.
About your father dying, I mean.'

There was a short, tense silence during which
neither looked at the other. Then Brad said
quietly, 'About what I said to you before I left
you in my cabin, I was still trying to warn you,
a little belatedly and after the fact, it's true,
but I wasn't blaming you for what happened.'

'And that riddle about oil and water not
mixing, what did you mean?' she asked
hopefully. At least he was communicating with
her, trying to explain.

'I was trying to tell you that there was no
future for us as lovers or as a couple. I'd tried
hard to keep you at a distance by being
unpleasant to you, by insulting you and by
flirting with Tizzy. I thought you'd get the
message when I didn't knock on your cabin
door that night you asked me to. It took a hell

of a lot of will-power on my part not to walk right in and take what you offered.' His voice rasped drearily. 'And then in Basseterre I was sure you'd turned off.' He gave a gruff laugh. 'But I didn't reckon on *you* coming to *my* cabin.'

He sat up again and rested both elbows on his knees. His hands, forming a peaked roof above his eyes, screened their expression.

'What happened that afternoon was something that has never happened to me before,' he murmured. 'Whenever I've indulged in any sexual activity with a woman I've liked I've always been in control. I've always been cool enough to lay down the guidelines and to direct the affair my way. All I can say now by way of an apology to you is that I shouldn't have let it happen. Since I left Morunda I've gone through hell worrying about you.'

'Why?'

'Can't you guess?' he dropped his hands. The burning intent expression in his eyes made her pulses leap.

For a few moments she wasn't in the cottage room but in the small fo'c'sle cabin on the *Montezuma* with the sound of rushing water all about her. The flare-up of passion between them had been sudden and beautiful, the wildest of wild impulses she had ever experienced in the whole of her impulsive life, and apparently it had been the same for him. What had happened had been perfect in every way, a meeting of minds as well as bodies, a complete fusion of their two entities, a mating . . . Her thoughts screeched to a stop. Wide-eyed she stared at him.

'You . . . you were worried in case you had made me pregnant?' she gasped.

'I was,' he agreed very seriously. 'There wasn't time for me to take precautions and I couldn't be sure of you . . .' He broke off as she shook her head negatively from side to side.

In a silence broken only by the patter of rain against the window they gazed at each other, their eyes dazed as if both of them had been caught and trapped by the memory of what had happened one steamy tropical afternoon in a small cabin; as if they were both wishing it was happening again.

CHAPTER ELEVEN

BRAD was the first to move and to break the silence. On his feet in one brisk movement, he paced away into the darkest corner of the room.

'So are you?' he demanded harshly, swinging round to look at her from the shadows.

'No, I'm not,' she replied. 'I wish I were but I'm not.'

'Thank God for small mercies,' he said on a surging breath of relief and paced back to her. 'But what do you mean by saying you wish you were?'

Clear-eyed, she looked up at him. A smile twitched at the corner of her lips.

'I wish I were, because if I were you'd have to marry me' she said tauntingly. 'That's why you were worried, isn't it? You've been afraid I might turn up at your door and insist that you marry me because I would be having your child.'

'No, damn you. That isn't why I was worried. I was concerned in case you did something desperate to get rid of it, but mostly I was afraid you would never tell me about it. You see, I know about that queer pride of yours and I also knew I hadn't given you any reason to believe I cared about what you did after I'd left Morunda. I was so bloody anxious I wrote to you.'

'You wrote me a letter?' she whispered. 'When?'

'Must have been beginning of March some time, when I guessed you would be back in Texas,' he replied, hands in his pockets as he paced around the room again.

'I came here on March 1st,' she said rather mournfully.

'I know. Your father told me that when he sent my letter to you back to me. He told me you were living and working at Greenacres Stables and asked me to look you up.' He paused in front of her again, slanted a derisive glance in her direction. Now that he had ascertained that she wasn't pregnant he seemed to have recovered his usual arrogance. 'He suggested I kept an eye on you, saw you didn't get into any mischief or take up with any undesirable characters,' he announced mockingly.

'Oh, hell.' The usual irritation with her father boiled through her. 'Why must he be so damned interfering? I came here to get away from his smothering all-protective attitude,' she raged. 'I came here to be independent, to prove to him and anyone else who cares to know that I'm not just a rich playgirl and that I don't want to be. So he had to write you and tell you where I am!' She broke off, her breast rising and falling as she still seethed with anger. He had walked away from her during her outburst and was picking up his jacket from the chairback over which he had hung it. He slipped it on.

'Where are you going?' she asked unsteadily.

'Back to London. I have to work tomorrow,' he said curtly. He zipped his jacket and strode towards the door. In a flash she was out of the

chair and had slid between him and the closed
door. Her back to the door, she faced him, her
chin up her head high, her loosened hair
shimmering like raw silk against the dark, oak
panelling of the old door.

'I'll see you again?' she asked. Although she
spoke in her usual, imperious rich-girl manner,
inside she was miserably aware that she had
offended him in some way and he had withdrawn
from her, just when he had seemed on the verge
of admitting he was in love with her.

'Not if you don't want to. Since you've just
made it very clear how you regard my keeping
an eye on you as your father suggested in his
letter, why should I hang around here?' he
retorted. 'He isn't paying me to be your
bodyguard any more, you know.'

'Mercenary,' she hissed.

'A guy makes his living the best way he can.
We aren't all born heirs or heiresses to a
fortune,' he jibed. 'Now, just stand aside,
Carlotta, and I'll be on my way.'

'Before you go you have to give me my letter,'
she insisted.

'What letter?' His face was impassive, the face
of an officer from an élite security force, trained
to be tough and watchful.

'The letter you wrote to me, of course.' She
held out one hand to him, palm upwards. 'Give
it to me.' If she could get it and read it she
might get some clue as to his real feelings about
her, she thought.

'I tore it up and threw it away,' he replied
blandly, looking her right in the eyes, his own
eyes absolutely without expression, dark, soulless.

'Oh, I guess you pass all the lie-detector tests

with flying colours. Get high grades all the time for lying without a flicker of an eyelid,' she sniped. Then, hands to her cheeks, she said more shakily, 'Oh, that was a mean thing to do out of the many mean things you've done and said, to write me a letter and then not let me have it, to tear it up and throw it away. It goes with you being glad that I'm not pregnant with your child.'

'I didn't say I'm glad you're not.' The breath he drew was sharp, giving her hope that her taunt had found a target.

'Relieved, then.'

His face was rigid, bone showing white along the angle of his jaw, lips a compressed line, eyelids lowered, a blind implacable face. Carlotta shivered. He seemed more like her enemy than her lover.

'Is there someone else?' she asked in a quieter, humbler way. 'If there is, if you have a woman already, hidden away somewhere in London, whom you love and to whom you're committed, I'll understand and I'll bow out of the picture as gracefully as I can.'

'There is no one else,' he replied slowly. 'There was once, but the affair ended when I asked her to marry me.'

'When you asked her . . .?' she exclaimed and broke off as surprise choked her voice. Wide-eyed she gazed up at him. Some of the hardness had gone from his face. One corner of his lips lifted in a familiar self-mocking smile. 'Why?' she croaked. 'Why did she turn you down?'

'She didn't like the job I was doing. I was in the security force then. She didn't like the violence involved, the guns I might have to use, the shift work.' He shrugged. 'There was a lot she didn't like about the job, but I think that really she had found out she didn't like me. She just used the job as an excuse to get out of the arrangement we had. She married someone else a month after we split.' The cynicism in his expression increased. 'Someone she could push around. Since then I haven't let myself become too serious about any woman. Short, casual affairs have been the order of the day.' He cocked a sardonic eyebrow. 'Got that?'

'Yes, I have. Very clearly. Another insult to add to the long list of insults you've handed out to me one way or another ever since I asked you to dance with me on New Year's Eve,' she raged.

His face took on its shuttered expression again. 'There's nothing to be gained by that sort of recrimination,' he retorted coldly. 'I'm sorry if you've felt insulted by anything I've said. Or done. I've tried to explain what I was doing, keeping you at a distance because there could be no future for us together.'

'The oil and water bit again?' she challenged jeeringly, and watched him closely. There was turbulence behind the impassivity. It was showing in the flare of red light in his eyes, in the twitch of a muscle at the corner of his mouth.

'Someone once put it better than I did,' he murmured. 'Someone once said rich girls don't marry poor boys.'

'And that's a lot of sentimental garbage,' she retorted, pushing away from the door and standing so close to him the tips of her breasts brushed against his jacket. Her eyes on the pulse beating madly at the base of his throat, she played with the zip of his jacket. 'Anyway, I'm not rich. I'm just a riding instructor at Greenacres Stables earning a few quid a week, and I'm still in love with you.' She glanced up at him through her lashes, half-smiling.

He didn't bend his stiff neck nor did he smile back at her but he closed his eyes so he couldn't see her.

'You're still Mason J. Burr's daughter and I thought I told you never to try it on again with me,' he said in his brisk Scotland Yard voice.

'But Dad isn't paying you any more. You don't owe him anything. No service, no loyalty,' she argued, and slid both hands around his neck to the nape. Her fingers enjoyed playing with his thick hair. 'As for me not trying it on again with you, what else can I do? It's the only weapon I have against your pride,' she whispered. 'I love you, Brad, I've had a few months away from you to find that out. I haven't changed my mind about you. I realised that when you walked into the tack-room yesterday. And I think you love me, just a tiny little bit, don't you?'

He answered her by kissing her as she had hoped he would, but as his hard lips claimed the softness of hers possessively and she leaned invitingly against him, they both heard the cottage door open, the high voice of Sarah followed by the deeper voice of Sarah's boyfriend Kenny.

Immediately Brad withdrew, raised his head and pushed her away. Alert and tense he slanted her an enquiring glance.

'It's only Sarah and Kenny. They won't come in here. Sarah has her own room,' she explained. 'Brad, don't go. Stay and have supper with me.

Stay the night. You can easily get to London from here in the morning.'

'You don't know what you're asking——' he started to argue roughly.

'Yes, I do. I'm asking you to stay and sleep with me. Oh, why do you persist in making it so hard for me?'

'Because you're right. I do love you,' he almost snarled at her, passion breaking through his control at last. 'Too much to have a casual affair with you. Too much to meet in secret. Too much to pretend . . .'

'Then why not ask me to marry you?' she interrupted him stormily.

He didn't bother to hide his scorn of her suggestion. It showed in the curl of his lower lip, in the way his glance raked her.

'I doubt if you could get by on my salary,' he jibed.

'Try me?' she challenged.

'No.'

They were facing each other like enemies again and she couldn't bear it. She flung herself at him, wrapping her arms around him, hiding her face against the tough leather of his jacket so that he wouldn't see the tears that had sprung to her eyes.

'How mean can you get?' she whispered unsteadily. 'How . . . how can I have your babies if . . . if you won't marry me?'

His chest rose and fell as he sighed. She felt his fingers in her hair, stroking it, then they were under her chin, forcing her face up so he could see it. She looked up, her own eyes starred with tears looking into his, which held a tortured

expression. With a forefinger he stroked away
one tear that had spilled on to her cheek.

'Blackmail?' he queried, with a lift of one
eyebrow.

'Yes. I . . . I'm very old-fashioned and I'm
not sleeping with you if I can't have a baby. I'm
not taking precautions and I never have.'

'Then I'd better leave right now.' Hands at
her waist he pushed her away again.

'*Brad!*' She almost screeched his name in her
agony. She caught hold of his arms and gripped
them hard. 'Oh, you'll be sorry if you go now,'
she went on in a low shaky voice. 'You'll be
really sorry if you leave me now and when they
tell you the next time you come to pick up
Joanna that I'm not here, that . . . that I've
done the Ophelia thing and drowned myself.'

Her voice faltered and tears brimmed again as
she saw his jaw was rigid. Letting go of him, she
turned away and trailed over to the settee. She
sank down on it and smoothed a hand over the
place where he had so recently sat, seeking
comfort from the warmth he had left there. 'It's
because I'm an heiress to Dad's loot, isn't it?'
she moaned. 'You don't want anyone to think
you're a fortune-hunter like Kurt.'

'That's part of it,' he admitted.

'And the other part?'

He swung round to face her, regarding her
from under frowning brows.

'My job. I'm not in the unit any more. I don't
have to go out with a gun to protect a place or
person where there's been a threat of a terrorist
attack. I'm in a more consultative, administrative
position, but I'm still involved with security. I
still deal in violence or, at least, the attempt to

prevent violence. And I like my job. I'm not
prepared to give it up.'

'I see.' Bitterness seared her. 'So I've to suffer
because my father is wealthy and some stupid
little girl, way back in your past, refused to
marry you because you were a security cop.
Thanks. Thanks a lot for that.' Her voice shook,
the tears spilled and she swayed against the back
of the settee, hands covering her face as she was
riven by a storm of emotion such as she had
never known before. 'Oh, God, what am I going
to do?' she muttered. 'I might as well be dead
if . . . if I can't live with you, be a part of your
life, no matter how unimportant.'

She didn't hear him stride across the room.
The first she knew that he was near to her was
the sinking of the settee cushions beneath his
weight when he sat beside her. Hands gentle on
her shoulders he lifted her away from the back
of the settee and held her to face him.

'You're not the only one who would suffer,'
he said unsteadily. 'Do you believe I wouldn't
suffer too, that I haven't already suffered . . .?'

'But why should we suffer?' she argued,
flinging back her head to look into his eyes.
'Why shouldn't we have each other, love each
other while we can?'

Her eyes brimmed again and he groaned.
Cupping her chin with one hand he kissed her
hard on the mouth, his lips pressing hers until
her own lips surrendered and parted to the
scorching heat of the kiss. Slowly his lips left
hers to kiss each tear away from her smooth,
golden cheeks with a tenderness she would never
forget. From her cheeks to her eyes his lips
wandered where he licked away the tears that

had not yet fallen, then from one temple to the
other before sliding down one cheek again to
the corner of her lips. With a long, sobbing sigh
she turned her head and their lips met again,
salt with her tears.

Against the back of the settee they leaned,
still kissing. From her waist to her breast his
hand moved, enclosing it with long tensile fingers.
At that tenderly marauding touch all her
frustrated love for him gushed forth. Her hands
became busy too, slipping undone shirt buttons,
sliding inside the shirt's opening, her fingers
curling against the mat of dark hairs, nails
digging into flesh that seemed to be on fire with
his desire.

Long ago in the cabin on the *Montezuma* they
hadn't spoken because no words had been
needed. No words were needed now. Anyway,
when they spoke to each other they said all the
wrong things, thought Carlotta dreamily, as he
lifted her in his arms and carried her through to
the dark bedroom.

Lying on the bed, they communicated through
hot, blistering kisses and subtly seeking caresses.
His warm fingers sliding over her bare skin sent
erotic sensations tingling through her and desire
began to swell slowly and pleasurably within her.

It was different from the swift, rocketing union
they had experienced on the yacht. There was
no panic, no lack of time, no fear that someone
might knock on the door. Every subtle caress
became a fulfilment in itself, was a pleasure to
be savoured, but inevitably the demand for
closer communication grew in both of them,
rising throbbingly until both of them were aware
no longer of where they were—in a yacht's cabin

with the sea rushing by or in a cottage bedroom on the creaking bed with the rain pattering at the window.

For a while, after it was done, they lay still and silent, she curled up with her back to him in the shelter of his arms. Only when she felt his fingers playing with her hair did she speak.

Softly, yet tauntingly she said, 'Now, you'll have to marry me.'

His answer was to kiss her shoulder, then the side of her neck, then her ear. She turned to face him, wishing she could see him.

'What does it matter who thinks you're a fortune-hunter as long as I know you're not,' she whispered. 'As long as I know you're not going to desert me when you find out that Dad has stopped my allowance and is changing his will so that his fortune will be spread out and I won't get everything. Anyway, he isn't going to die for years and years yet. Given his health and vitality he'll probably live until he's over ninety and it'll be our children who'll inherit everything. As for your job, I don't mind about that. I know you're doing something that is necessary these days. I'll hate it only when it takes you away from me, but I intend to go on working here, at the stables, for as long as I can, and I'm willing to put up with being separated from you for short periods of time because separation will make getting together so much more exciting. I promise you, you'll never get bored being my *real* husband!'

His mouth claiming hers again in hard possession stifled the rest of her running commentary, and happily she submitted again to the mastery of his love-making until, through the tumultuous sound of her heart in her ears, she thought she heard a voice calling to her. Sarah's high soprano. It was near. In the next room!

Sitting up sharply Carlotta gasped, 'Sarah!' and then bounded from the bed. She snatched her dressing-gown from the curtain-covered clothes alcove, wrapped it around herself and darted into the living-room, closing the door on the sound of Brad's muffled laughter.

Sarah, pink-cheeked from hovering over a cooker, was standing in the middle of the living-room staring at Brad's jacket, which he had tossed carelessly over the arm of the settee.

'What do you want?' Carlotta demanded.

'I . . . oh.' Startled, Sarah looked away from the jacket and at Carlotta. Her wide, china-blue eyes widened even more as she noted Carlotta's tangled hair, poppy-red bruised lips, hastily donned dressing-gown and bare feet. 'Kenny and I are having spaghetti and meat sauce for supper and I don't have any basil or Parmesan cheese. Could I borrow them from you?' As if drawn by a magnet, Sarah's eyes swerved back to the incriminating man's jacket.

'Yes, I have.' Carlotta went quickly to the cooking alcove opened a wall cupboard, searched for and found both basil and Parmesan. She thrust them at Sarah who was still mesmerised by the jacket. 'There you are. Now, go. I can smell your sauce burning.'

'Oh, gosh.' Whirling, Sarah ran for the door, but looked back before she closed it and added impishly, 'You look awfully pretty, Carlo, when you've been kissed.'

The door slammed shut and the cushion that

Carlotta had grabbed and flung at Sarah fell to the floor, never having reached its target. For a second Carlotta stood glaring at the door, fuming inwardly, then slowly she began to grin, remembering her own hasty rush from the bedroom. As if it mattered that Sarah had guessed she had been with a lover in the bedroom! Neither Sarah nor Kenny made a secret of their relationship. They did everything up front.

'So what do you have in mind for *my* supper tonight? drawled Brad from the bedroom doorway and she turned to look at him. He was buttoning his shirt.

'You're going to stay then?' she said hopefully, going over to him.

'Only for supper . . . and then I must go.'

'But you'll . . . you'll come again, next weekend . . . or even during the week.' She put her arms around him and rested her head against his chest. 'I . . . I'll be a very good wife. I've been well trained by my grandmother. I'll always be here when you need me. I like cooking and I'm pretty good at it . . .'

'So how about proving that now,' he murmured. 'I'm ravenous!'

'OK!'

He went back into the bedroom and she went to search cupboards for food, singing softly to herself. She had won. She had overcome his stubborn resistance. She heard him come back into the room and, checking that the food she was preparing was cooking, she went over to the table and began to set it.

'When we're married,' she began.

'I haven't asked you yet,' he said softly and she flinched giving him a wide wary glance.

'But . . . but . . .' She stammered and stopped. 'I'm sorry,' she went on more humbly. 'I tend to jump ahead and . . . and . . .'

'Make assumptions,' he supplied. 'That's because you're used to having your own way.' She must have looked crestfallen because he came over to her and smiled down at her. 'Don't worry, sweetheart. I'm going to ask you to marry me, but in my own way and when I'm ready. It's going to take me a while to adjust to the idea and then there is the matter of having to write to Mason J. Burr.'

'This has nothing to do with him. Nothing at all,' she said tautly.

'Will you let me finish?' he admonished her gently, yet sternly. 'The way I propose marriage, it has a lot to do with him. You claim to be old-fashioned. Well, I claim to be a traditionalist and although I know it isn't considered to be necessary these days, I'm going to write to Mason to tell him we're going to be married and to ask for his blessing. It will show him courtesy and respect and will perhaps convince him I'm not a fortune-hunter.' He smiled at her again. 'Please bear with me, love. I am what I am and it's too late in the day for me to change my ways.'

He touched her cheek with one finger. She grabbed and held the finger then pressed his hand against her lips for a second.

'Dad said you're a nice guy and I agree with him,' she said. 'I'll bear with you. I'll put up with your rocklike pride, your cynicism, your reserve and your job as long as you'll hold me in your arms often, sometimes kiss me, keep me safe and say you love me.'

'I love you, capricious Carlotta,' he said, his voice unsteady. 'I've loved you from the day I first set eyes on you in Morunda,' he confessed. 'It's just been hard to believe that you love me in the same way. Even now . . . I can't be sure that you won't change your mind about me once we're married.'

Shaken by his confession, and dismayed by his lack of confidence in her, Carlotta did the only thing she could: she showed her affection by flinging her arms around him and kissing him, but because they kissed too long supper wasn't the success she had planned. The steaks were overdone and the sauce burned. By the time Brad got up from the table to go she was almost in tears again, convinced he wouldn't come back because he didn't like her cooking.

Following him to the door, she said urgently, 'I don't know where you live. I have no address or telephone number. I don't know how to get in touch with you if . . . if I need to.'

He turned back to her, slanted her a thoughtful glance and slowly put his hand in the slit pocket of his jacket and brought out a rather crumpled envelope. He handed it to her.

'My address and telephone number are in that.' As she took it from him he bent and kissed her temple. 'See you, soon, lover,' he whispered.

He went while she was still staring at the envelope. It was addressed to herself at the Burr ranch in Texas. It was the letter he had written to her. The devil had lied to her when he had said he had torn it up and thrown it away! Her heart jumping, she went over to the armchair, curled up in it, slit the envelope open and took out the single page of notepaper.

'My dear Carlotta,' she read, and could hear his voice in her ears, soft and deep as it had been when he had admitted to loving her. 'I had to leave the yacht and fly home without saying goodbye to you,' the letter continued, going straight to the point. 'That's bothering the hell out of me. I can't help thinking you must believe I'm a complete bastard for not having more control when you came to my cabin. The truth is, sweetheart, I have never felt for any woman what I felt for you at that moment in time. Your beauty, the heat, your closeness to me in that small cabin were too much for me. I gave in to the longing I had to love you and, well, you know what happened.

'No one knows more than I do that a great gulf separates us. You're a wealthy heiress accustomed to having everything you want, everything money can buy. You've been sheltered and protected all your life. You're lovely, naïve and innocent. My background has been very different and I am none of the things you are, but I guessed early on in our acquaintance that Kurt had been rough with you, and I felt compassion for you. I could have killed him, if he hadn't been dead already, for violating you.

'But to get back to the reason for this letter. Please write and let me know how you are. We both behaved recklessly that afternoon without thought for any consequences. The thought now that you are pregnant and possibly considering doing something to get rid of the pregnancy is making me sweat with horror. Please write and tell me the truth about yourself and don't do anything before I come to you. Sincerely, Brad.'

For a long time Carlotta sat with the letter in her hand. Now she knew she was truly loved by the man she loved. It was the driving force of passionate love that had made him write this letter, had made him drop the barrier of his cool reserve and admit that he cared about what happened to her and about what had happened during her day-long marriage to Kurt.

The letter convinced her that Brad would be back, but she had to wait three long weeks before she saw him again. During that time she received a phone call from Texas, from Mason telling her that he had received a letter from Brad asking his permission to propose marriage to her.

'So what are you going to do?' she asked cautiously.

'I've written back to say I'll be happy to attend your wedding to him whenever you decide to have the ceremony,' he replied, equally cautious.

'Oh, Dad, thank you, thank you, thank you!' Carlotta couldn't stay cautious for long.

Not having heard from Brad she was thinking she would have to go up to London to find him when he turned up one Saturday afternoon at the stables.

'I've come for Joanna,' he said. 'And also to ask you out to dinner. The time has come for me to propose.' He glanced around the stableyard where girls were heaving saddles off horses and shouting to each other. Looking back at her, he suddenly lost his casual pose. Little red sparks began to flare in his eyes as he stepped close to her. 'I was going to do it over candlelight and wine glasses, to soft music,' he murmured. 'But I can't wait any longer.' He grasped both of her hands in his. 'Will you marry me, Carlotta of the golden eyes and golden hair, and will you have my babies?'

The mockery that rippled through his voice and danced in his eyes didn't offend her because she knew now that it hid the burning sincerity of his love for her.

'Oh, Tristan,' she mocked back, 'I thought you'd never ask.' Then sobering, she looked up at him all the love she felt for him expressed in her eyes. 'I'll marry you with pleasure,' she whispered.

Heedless of the curious stares of the suddenly silent girls, he swept her against him and kissed her hard and she kissed him back, thankful that there was no need for pretence or secrecy, that the masquerade begun on a wild impulse months ago was going to become a reality at last.

Take
4 novels
and a
surprise gift
FREE

FREE BOOKS/GIFT COUPON

Mail to **Harlequin Reader Service®**

In the U.S.
901 Fuhrmann Blvd.
P.O. Box 1394
Buffalo, N.Y. 14240-1394

In Canada
P.O. Box 609
Fort Erie, Ontario
L2A 5X3

YES! Please send me 4 free Harlequin Superromance® novels and my free surprise gift. Then send me 4 brand-new novels every month as they come off the presses. Bill me at the low price of $2.74 each*—a 7% saving off the retail price. There are no shipping, handling or other hidden costs. There is no minimum number of books I must purchase. I can always return a shipment and cancel at any time. Even if I never buy another book from Harlequin, the 4 free novels and the surprise gift are mine to keep forever.   134 BPS BP7F

*Plus 49¢ postage and handling per shipment in Canada.

Name	(PLEASE PRINT)

Address	Apt. No.

City	State/Prov.	Zip/Postal Code

This offer is limited to one order per household and not valid to present subscribers. Price is subject to change.   ILSR-SUB-1B

ATTRACTIVE, SPACE SAVING BOOK RACK

Display your most prized novels on this handsome and sturdy book rack. The hand-rubbed walnut finish will blend into your library decor with quiet elegance, providing a practical organizer for your favorite hard-or soft-covered books.

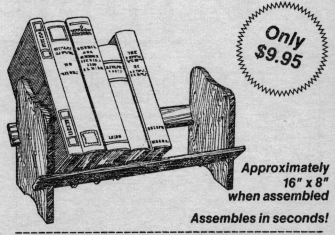

Only $9.95

Approximately 16" x 8" when assembled

Assembles in seconds!

To order, rush your name, address and zip code, along with a check or money order for $10.70* ($9.95 plus 75¢ postage and handling) payable to *Harlequin Reader Service*:

> Harlequin Reader Service
> Book Rack Offer
> 901 Fuhrmann Blvd.
> P.O. Box 1396
> Buffalo, NY 14269-1396

Offer not available in Canada.

*New York and Iowa residents add appropriate sales tax.

BKR-1A

Harlequin Presents

Coming Next Month

1031 WINTER SUNLIGHT Susan Alexander
Sophie can't believe it. Max is offering her what she most wants. But marriage with Max, an eminent Austrian baron, is not for her. She can love him, have an affair with him. But not marriage!

1032 NIGHT OF THE CONDOR Sara Craven
Crossing the world to join her fiancé in Peru changes spoiled wealthy Leigh Frazier's life. For in meeting the fascinating archeologist Dr. Rourke Martinez, she is drawn under the spell of the high Andes, in a new and dangerous embrace....

1033 THE ONE THAT GOT AWAY Emma Darcy
Substituting as skipper on her father's fishing boat, chartered by American football player and movie star, Taylor Marshall, Jillian realizes after she falls in love, that to him it's just another game. And will she be just another trophy?

1034 SINGLE COMBAT Sandra Field
Lydia grew up without love. She's learned to live without it, she thinks. Now here's James who simply refuses to be put off like the other men who had proposed marriage. If she could only let herself trust him....

1035 IF LOVE BE BLIND Emma Goldrick
Penn Wilderman, suffering from temporary snow blindness, is convinced by her manner that Philomena Peabody, who's looking after him, is a sweet little old lady. This doesn't worry Phil, until in order to win a custody battle for his son, Penn asks Phil to marry him!

1036 DON'T ASK FOR TOMORROW Susanne McCarthy
Kate hires skipper Sean McGregor to help prove that her late husband had discovered the wreck, the *Belle Etoile*. Sean had worked with her husband, and guards a secret concerning him. But Kate soon discovers that she must give up the past—or betray her love.

1037 TANGLED HEARTS Carole Mortimer
Love, hate, loyalty all mix in Sarah's mind. She wants to run. But no matter what it costs, she can't let anyone else in her family be denied love because of Garrett Kingham—and her fear of facing him again.

1038 ELDORADO Yvonne Whittal
Gina's schoolgirl crush on Jarvis had long been replaced by a more mature emotion. She is woman enough now to know that her feelings are somehow being manipulated. And she can't help wondering if Jarvis is really interested in her—or just in her property.

Available in December wherever paperback books are sold, or through Harlequin Reader Service:

In the U.S.
901 Fuhrmann Blvd.
P.O. Box 1397
Buffalo, N.Y. 14240-1397

In Canada
P.O. Box 603
Fort Erie, Ontario
L2A 5X3

For the millions who can't read
Give the Gift of Literacy

One out of five adults in North America
cannot read or write well enough
to fill out a job application
or understand the directions on a bottle of medicine.

You can change all this by joining the fight
against illiteracy.

For more information write to:
Contact, Box 81826, Lincoln, Neb. 68501
In the United States, call toll free: 1-800-228-8813

The only degree you need
is a degree of caring

"This ad made possible with the cooperation of the Coalition for Literacy and the Ad Council."
Give the Gift of Literacy Campaign is a project of the book and periodical industry,
in partnership with Telephone Pioneers of America.